Linnea March

Contents

Also by Linnea March   V

Dedication   VI

1. Chapter 1   1
2. Chapter 2   8
3. Chapter 3   23
4. Chapter 4   38
5. Chapter 5   49
6. Chapter 6   67
7. Chapter 7   79
8. Chapter 8   93
9. Chapter 9   100
10. Chapter 10   114
11. Chapter 11   121
12. Chapter 12   134
13. Chapter 13   144
14. Chapter 14   154

15. Chapter 15   158

16. Chapter 16   162

17. Chapter 17   170

18. Chapter 18   182

19. Chapter 19   194

20. Chapter 20   206

21. Epilogue   214

Acknowledgements   220

About the Author   221

Also by Linnea March

Prevalent Notion Series

Faultless Notion

Treacherous Notion

Ruinous Notion

Reckless Liar

The One You Chose

To Rusty for making the best breakfast every time

Ask Me Why I Love You

Ask me why I love you, dear,
   And I will ask the rose
Why it loves the dews of Spring
   At the Winter's close;
Why the blossoms' nectared
sweets
   Loved by questing bee,—
I will gladly answer you,
   If they answer me.

Ask me why I love you, dear,
   Let the lark reply,
Why his heart is full of song
   When the twilight's nigh;
Why the lover heaves a sigh
   When her heart is true;
If you will but answer me,
   I will answer you.

Walter Everette Hawkins

Wren

IT FIGURES THAT THE first car accident of my life was because of a missed turn. After all, missing a turnoff had to be my most consistent talent. Seven years in dance had led to nothing but the ability to pick up things with my toes and a tendency to break tasks down into eight counts. I had the gift of baking passable macrons and found the perfect red lipstick for my olive skin tone. But if I was known for one thing, it was always—without fail—missing the turnoffs.

My ex-boyfriend, Buck, never let me drive, citing the little three-point detours we had to take with every trip.

The whole way up the long trip, I was careful not to miss this turn. But all the tree-named streets sounded the same: Cedar Drive, Aspen Avenue, Sitka Lane.

Sitka, that was the one.

Slamming on my brakes, my little sedan skidded through the soft snow, veering to the right, where the front bumper wedged into a snowdrift. My head snapped forward, hitting the steering wheel, before whipping back into my headrest. Between the bang and my jostled body, I heard my chip bag crunch as my soda rolled over it.

Little spots formed behind my eyes as I blinked at the snowbank before me. Air rasped in my throat as I took my shaking hands off the steering wheel and patted myself down to check for injuries. Arms still attached, stomach still squishy, boobs still boobing. A wince shot through me as I touched my forehead. Blood clung to my finger. Flipping the mirror down, I looked at my reflection. A small but angry-looking cut at my hair line bled slowly. I grabbed a brown TacoTime napkin from the center console and dabbed the gash. It had stopped bleeding, but a knot was forming underneath.

Great.

I threw the napkin on the crushed chip bag, knowing its contents would be tiny little bits. A sign I shouldn't be eating chips in the car.

Buck's words echo in my head.

If you watch what you eat, maybe you'll lose this junk you're carrying around.

Asshole.

How did it take me so long to see it? And, worst of all, why did he get to be the one to dump me instead of the other way around? If there were anything more embarrassing than being dumped after three years together, it had to be by a guy you didn't even liked in the first place.

Are your chips really the big issue here, Wren?

Damn. No, of course not.

I stuck my car in reverse and hit the gas, only to hear the loud whir of my tires but feel no movement. The steering wheel was cold against my palms, and I shook the wheel while letting out a scream through my teeth.

I tried to think back to driver's ed. What would old Ms. Crawford say about this situation? She would, likely, be unsurprised. It took me five tries to pass my driver's test. I suspected the fine people at Ridgewood Drivers' Education were tired of seeing my face. And yet, I had never been in an accident—until today. Alone, in the Olympic Mountains, miles away from the closest town of Icicle Creek and many more from the nearest Nordstrom.

My phone chimed with a text, and I glanced at it.

Him. Again. This time it was, *Where did you put my snowshoes?*

If Buck had a talent, it was picking the worst time to ask for something. Did he have a superpower to sense when I was at my lowest?

I responded to Buck with the location, in the attic, beside his hiking gear he never wore and under the expensive tent he used once.

He sent back a red heart emoji. That man dumps me and then sends me hearts? Heat prickled beneath my skin.

The trip was supposed to be my birthday present from Buck, and our first time away together, just the two of us. Every other one we took ended up with a gaggle of his buddies tagging along—or worse, his family. When I made the reservation, Buck told me he'd call them to put his credit card down for the deposit.

This morning, I'd awoken to an email confirming the reservation starting tonight and the full charge of the stay on my already stressed credit card. Nonrefundable, nontransferable.

Still in my old Ridgewood High jazz choir tee shirt and covered in my Grandma Pearl's afghan, I made the split decision to head up to the cabin myself.

My parent's house was far too quiet since they decided to visit my aunt in California for the long winter weekend.

You sure you don't want to come with us, Wren? I'm sure Cathy would fix up the dogs' room with a trundle bed.

No, thank you. I may be twenty-four, newly dumped, and currently staying in my childhood bedroom, but I drew the line at sleeping in the room my aunt used for her five Akitas.

I had given little thought to the weather, what I had thrown into my enormous suitcase, or how well my 2015 Toyota Corolla would do in the snowy mountains. All I needed was to get out of my childhood bedroom and away from the stink of failure following me.

I sent a message to my best friend, Summer, who was likely packing for her internship in London and wouldn't see it for hours. I also messaged my parents, saying that I was going to spend the long weekend in Icicle Creek. My mother's response, *Have fun with your friends*, had made me laugh.

Yeah, I could be my own friend.

The service here was spotty, but the road I had carelessly tried to brake for was the one I needed. My boots made tracks in the fresh snow as I walked to the top of Sitka Lane, assessing how far I'd have to go with my suitcase to get to the log cabin. I was pleased to see it only a short distance away, exactly like the picture in my email. I could walk that far.

Pulling on my favorite pink beanie, careful not to touch my injury, I grabbed my bag but left the smashed potato chips. Once I got to the cabin, I would use the provided Wi-Fi and arrange for a tow truck. That's what people did in these situations, right? I am a smart, independent woman who doesn't need her asshole boyfriend to carry her bags.

Halfway up the road, my suitcase slipping from my hand every two feet, doubt of my independent abilities crept in. Sweat dripped down my back, and I shrugged off my thick coat to stuff it into my luggage. The only sound on the street was a light birdsong and the crunch of the new white boots I bought for a trip to Aspen. The one Buck said he was going to take me on the previous Valentine's Day. That fell through when he, instead, went with three of his buddies from high school.

You understand, right, Wrenny? I love how cool you are, not at all like those other girls my friends have for girlfriends.

Annoyance fizzed through me as I picked up my bag again, the motivator I needed to make it. While it was likely only five minutes after I left my car, it felt like thirty before I got to the cabin's driveway. I slipped twice, my gloves getting soaked in the powdery snow.

The road ended in a high snowbank, with two identical log cabins on each side. The one I was facing had a green door, the one behind me a red door. Both two-story, with a porch spanning the width of the house. Each had a high-pitched roof for the snow to fall from and a small balcony on the second floor. This had to be it. There were only two houses at the end of Sitka Lane.

Hoisting my suitcase up on the patio, I pulled out my phone to check the address against the number in the email. 143 Sitka.

I was expecting the key to be in the lockbox next to the door, but I hadn't come across it yet. The wind was cooling me off from my hike. My thin white sweater was no match for the winter air. Another text came though as I read the instructions. This time, it was Buck asking for the recipe for my deviled eggs. The ones I made every year and he accepted praise for.

It was the first one that popped up on Google. You'd think an accountant for a Fortune 500 company could figure out how to search on the Internet.

Ignoring his text, I walked around the building, looking for the lockbox and finding nothing on the wall. A large outdoor chest sat on the edge of the porch beside a pile of perfectly stacked wood in a wrought iron holder. Across the expanse of the wall, a big window showcased a darkened room. A leather couch sat behind an oversized green rug with a fireplace in the middle of the wall. In the distance, a few bulky jackets hung from a pine wood rack. Must be from the previous guests. The starkly tidy house lacked little touches of a lived-in space, with generic scenery pictures identical to the landscape outside and a single framed picture of an older couple.

Stepping back from the window, I glanced again at the numbers on the house and the email. This was it, 143 Sitka.

The door had a keypad on it. Maybe that was the code I was supposed to use. On the porch again, I tried the code to get a flashing red light. After a second time, the red light glared brighter.

A glance across the street at the other house had me hesitate. That house didn't have numbers posted, and this was the right address. It was the only one that came up on my navigation in all of Washington State.

At the bottom of the letter was the phone number to call if there were any issues. I clicked on the number and watched the screen as it tried to connect, tried, tried. Call failed. Sure, service would be spotty up here, but why have a number if I couldn't get in?

A third time yielded the same results. Great, Buck's little plea for deviled eggs goes through, but my rescue can't. Got it.

As I was about to try again, an engine rumbled down the street, and a large white truck pulled into the driveway. I huffed a sigh of relief. This had to be the owner. Who else could it be? She must have realized she had given me the wrong code and had come to let me in.

The driver turned the truck off, a sudden quiet falling over the street. The door opened, and I set my phone on top of my oversized suitcase and trudged the stairs to the truck. "Hi! Are you Agatha? I can't get into the house with the code and..."

A long leg swung out from the seat, followed by a second.

It was a man. A muscular man. He stomped toward me, and I took a step back.

Alone on this snowy road, with no streetlights, and my car parked too far forward in the snowdrift, I should have been worrying about this man being a serial killer. But damn if he wasn't the most handsome man I had ever seen. He didn't appear to be much older than me, maybe in his late twenties. Dark hair peeked out of his hat, over the greenest blue eyes fringed with long thick lashes. He had a mouth that was full and soft. A mouth that was currently frowning at me.

"Oh, I'm guessing you're not Agatha."

"No, I'm not," he grunted out, running a hand over his unshaven face. Thumbing behind him, he pointed to the house on the other side of the road. "Agatha's house is there. You're some visitor renting the cabin?"

Okay, so not a serial killer, probably. A helpful serial killer? An extremely hot, helpful serial killer.

No, this guy didn't look helpful. He looked annoyed.

As the handsome man approached me, his grim face and narrowed eyes gave me the sinking feeling that maybe I should have kept going when I missed my turn.

Adrian

FEW THINGS TASTED BETTER after a long day on the mountain than a good beer. I had the requisite tall can in the parking lot with my friends before we parted ways, our snow pants rolled down around our waists, and the sweat from a hard ride still damp under our beanies. We all grabbed a can out of the small cooler in Tam's trunk. It had been a tradition—as far back as I remember—that the last person to our meeting spot in the morning supplied the beer for after our runs. And every week, it was always Tam. Cracking open the tall can, I took my first swig as a young woman approached our group, her blue eyes on me.

"Hey, could I ask you to help me with my rack?" She thumbed behind her at a Subaru parked five spots down with a set of skis leaning against the door. "The lock is sticky."

Tam grabbed the can out of my hand and pushed me forward. "He'd be delighted."

I followed her past two high schoolers smoking pot inside their truck and a father trying to wrestle his kid out of a snowsuit without getting their feet wet.

While studying the rack, I put out a gloved hand. "You got the key?"

She handed me the small key, and it slid right into the lock.

"You ski here often?" she asked. I watched as she leaned against the back of the car, pulling on her long blond braid. Her jacket was unzipped, exposing the tight thermal she wore underneath.

"I board." With a quick turn of the key, the arm of the rack swung up.

"My ex boarded. Or he tried." She laughed at her own joke.

Grabbing her skis, I slid them in place and closed the arm back down on them. "That was easy. I bet you could have done it yourself."

Her smile fell, and she glanced at my group of friends behind me. "Right. Um, thanks, Mr. Winter."

Frowning, I placed a hand on the top of her car and looked her over. "Do I know you?"

She stepped back, zipping her coat up to her throat. "Yeah, Layla Parsons. I was in your American literature class five years ago?"

With a furrowing of my brow, I rustled through the hundreds of students over the years. Icicle Creek High wasn't a large school, but I tended to forget most students after they graduated unless they made a big impression on me. "Yeah, Layla. How are you?"

"You don't remember me." She let out a shaky breath. "Nice move, dumbass."

"No, I do—" I grimaced. "Kind of. I'm sorry. Unless you blew up a trashcan, I forget names."

Shaking her head, she stared up at the white-and-gray sky. "God, I had such a big crush on you throughout school, and you don't even remember my name."

As one of the younger members of the faculty, I had my share of students staying behind a little too long to ask me questions, twirling their hair, or stepping too close.

"Ah." I sucked at my teeth. "I'm sure, once you got out into the real world, that faded fast, and you realized I'm just some boring old dude."

A sly smile ticked at the corner of her mouth. "I wouldn't say that. I'm twenty-one now. You're, what, thirty-two?"

"Twenty-nine," I answered hesitantly.

"Only eight little years between us. It was a big deal when I was seventeen, but now—"

I stepped back, shaking my head. "It was nice to see you, Layla. Tell your folks I said hi." I had no clue who her parents were, but I had to step away.

"Maybe I'll see you at The Horse and Trails!" she shouted at my retreating back. "I'll be there tonight with friends!"

Walking back to my friends, I took my beer back from Tam as the group silently stared at me. Taking a long swig, I was met with only silence. "What?"

My friends chimed on top of each other.

"Dude."

"What the fuck, man."

"You are the dumbest mofo ever."

Pulling off my glove, I tossed it into my truck beside us. "Me?"

"Ad, come on." With a shake of his head, Tam glanced at our friends, and I had a feeling he was about to say something they had discussed many times over. "That girl was into you."

"No way. She needed help with her rack. I helped her."

"She came over here, didn't glance at any of us—only you—and asked for help on a brand-new Thule rack?"

I swallowed against my thick tongue. They loved taking jabs at each other, and to give them this ammunition was too easy. "She was a student. I can't...go there." I put my hands up to emphasize my point. With a glance, I saw her pulling out of the parking lot, skis secure on her roof. "It's not right."

"She's not your student now, is she? Because she looked legal," Clark asked.

"She's twenty-one, but it's still weird. I was her teacher."

"Many a hot video starts out that way," Clark ribbed. The guys laughed, and I groaned. Why didn't I tell them I wasn't into her? Would have been simpler.

"That's between you, your hand, and your sticky computer screen." I pulled off my hat, throwing it in the bed of my truck.

"Look at you with the standards all of a sudden. Last I checked, you'd fuck anything with tits." Clark laughed big enough that I could see the fillings in the back of his mouth.

"Ignore them." Tam clapped me on the shoulder. "It's cool, man. There'll be another one who comes around. I should introduce you to Jessie. I bet she'd like to go out with you."

"You did, remember? We went on that double date in October. She said she could tell I wasn't into something serious like she was."

Tam frowned. "Oh, right."

I couldn't fault my friends for trying. Were there quite a few tourist hookups over the years? Sure, meeting a cute girl at The Horse and Trails and bringing her back to my small apartment in town was frequent enough when I was fresh out of college. As young guys, we all had our wild times of hookups and late nights. Slowly, my friends settled down, got wives, or at least long-term girlfriends. Tam found Penny, who I adored like a sister. I was never hurting in the one-night stand area, but anything longer than three dates fizzled out before it went anywhere. All the women in town, I knew and had experienced my share of them. Maybe I should have been pickier as a young man, but I was young and stupid. Did I deserve the man whore reputation I built? Maybe.

At the time, it all seemed to be in good fun. Why settle down with a girl from town when there were so many options coming in every weekend for recreation? My parents never minded me being away for long periods, partying, and coming home with girls. Why should they? Both were busy with their work in real estate, selling luxury second homes to out-of-towners. I think they were happy to have one less person in the house, leaving drink stains on the table and eating all their food. The moment I graduated from college, they replaced my bed with a Pilates machine and my shelf of books with a floor-to-ceiling mirror. If I needed to stay over at their house, I was stuck with the foldout in the living room.

But my grandparents always had a room for me.

Sweethearts from their first meeting when Gran walked into the attendance office on her first day of high school and Gramps offered to walk her to her first class. He used to tell everyone, "The second I saw my Winifred, it was over. She was the prettiest thing I had ever seen. Never looked at another woman."

They were married for sixty-one years.

Even a year later, losing them within months of each other was the single most devastating event of my life. I took little solace out of inheriting their house. My parents wouldn't have wanted it, too small, too far from town, and far too rustic for their tastes. I moved out of my bachelor apartment above the bar in town and into the cabin in the mountains that had always felt like the truest home I had. With the move came an abrupt change in me. I was nearly thirty, with only my dog to keep me company. While I didn't need to find a wife right away, the stark truth was, the last relationship I had that lasted longer than three weeks was in middle school.

The first night at the cabin, I lay in my old room and realized for the first time how lonely my life had become. It was too much to expect to see someone and fall for them right away, the way my grandfather did, but shouldn't I be open to the possibility of something serious?

But Icicle Creek had other plans. The women I had previous dalliances with were already in relationships or completely unsuitable. And now, I'm being propositioned by a girl who, last I saw, had braces and Pokémon stickers on her binder.

"Man, I don't know what's the matter with you. Truitt Baker can't weigh more than a buck fifty, has a rat tail, and that guy always has a new girlfriend."

"Thanks," I grumbled into my tall can.

"You know what I mean. You are way better looking than even me, and I bagged the hottest girl in town."

"Yeah, but he has to actually talk to a woman in the morning if he wants one to stick around," Clark joked.

My friends all laughed around me. I responded with a halfhearted smirk to let them know I wasn't offended. They weren't wrong.

"It's not that hard to talk to girls. They're women, not a mathematical equation."

Maybe if they were, I'd have an easier time.

"Ask them about themselves—tell them they look pretty in the color they're wearing. They eat that shit up."

With one hand, I crumbled the can in my hand, tossing it into the small plastic bag in the back of Tam's truck.

"I got to dip. Maizie is getting hungry."

"Now there's a female you'll commit to." Clark laughed. "Too bad it's a terrier."

Ignoring my friends, I climbed into my truck, ready to head the twenty minutes back to my place in the woods. As good as that tall boy lager was, what I really craved was my favorite Hazy IPA from nearby Icicle Brewing. Driving down my road, I spied a car stuck in a snowdrift to the side. Some people had no idea how to drive in the snow. A peek in the window as I passed told me there was no one in the car. Good. Hopefully, they called someone. Shaking my head, I continued down Sitka Lane into my driveway on the right. As I pulled into my driveway, I could practically taste the hoppy goodness on my tongue.

That wish died out as I spied a lone figure standing on my front porch, bathed in the yellowy flickering light I meant to switch to an LED bulb. Beside the woman—yes, on closer inspection, it was clearly a woman—was a large suitcase. A bright pink beanie with two white puffs like mouse ears covered brown curly hair in two braids. She was short. I could see that much, far shorter than me. The woman was wearing a bright white coat. No, not a coat, dear God, it was...a sweater. She was standing on the doorstep wearing a thin sweater. It couldn't be over thirty degrees Fahrenheit outside, and this woman was on my porch, jiggling my doorknob, freaking out my dog, and looking in my windows. In a summer sweater. As I cut the lights, the woman turned to face me.

I sucked in a breath at her. She had large warm eyes and a smattering of freckles across her nose and full lips. Her face brightened as she saw my car. My stomach pitched at the warmth of her expression. It had been a long time since I reacted that way to a simple smile. In the town of Icicle Creek, I knew everyone's face, but this one—this was bright and cheery, and damn if I didn't feel a little funny from it.

"Hi!" She made her way down the front porch. "Are you Agatha? I can't get into the house with the code and..."

Her sentence dropped off as I climbed out of the car, standing a head above her.

"Oh, I'm guessing you're not Agatha." She took a step back, her grin dropping.

"No, I'm not," I grunted out, my voice more gravelly than normal. Did I strain it on the mountain? Why did it sound like that? No taking it back now. Best to get this woman off my porch so I could spend my evening in solitude. She was obviously a tourist, and while I had my share of tourists in my apartment in town, I had never brought someone back to my grandparent's cabin. I pointed at the house across the street. "Agatha's house is there. You're some visitor renting the cabin?"

My neighbor, Agatha Dawes, was a pleasant woman, but technology had never been her strong suit. No matter how many times I told her I would help her fix her vacation listing, my address was still the one that was listed. Her frequent trips down to Nevada in the winter to visit her daughter meant I was often stuck with wayward travelers. On a normal day, I might be more willing to help, but something about this woman set me on edge. Who did she think she was standing on my porch—in a thin sweater and large suitcase, with her too-bright smile and eyes so warm they made my cheeks heat—jiggling my doorknob?

"Yeah, was it the suitcase that gave me away?" She put out her hand. "Wren Alexander."

Wren. It fit her. Small bird. I took her hand, the softness of her palm sending shivers up my arm. "Adrian Winter."

"Winter. In the winter." Her smile quirked at the corner.

"Little Bird lost." I quipped back. I wasn't sure why I said that. While I flirted with women at bars, come-ons on my front porch were a bad idea. Plus, the line sounded cheesy at best.

She wrapped her thin sweater around her body, hiding what I could tell was a lush body. I trained my eyes not to look at her cleavage. She seemed to be waiting for me to say something. On her feet were white pristine snow boots with fuzzy stuff coming out of the top. I wondered if this was the first snowflake they had seen.

A rush of annoyance ran through me. I hated those snow boots and needed this woman away from me. Pushing past her, I stomped up the front steps and grabbed the handle of her suitcases, lifting them up.

I ignored the "Oh my" comment from the woman and made my way across the street. I was almost on the front porch of the other cabin before I realized that the woman wasn't following me.

"Are you coming or not?" I barked, setting the suitcase under the porch and walking back to the middle of the road.

She scurried behind me, slipping slightly on the patches of black ice on the street. The snowplow didn't make its way down my road, so it was up to me to shovel the snow away.

"Careful. Slow down." I wasn't normally this bossy. Well, okay, maybe I was. But typically, that tone was reserved for my students at the high school, not for beautiful out-of-towners who were very obviously not in high school.

"I'm fine. I do all my own stunts." The smile she gave me as she jumped over a snow pile set off an odd feeling in my stomach. I shouldn't have eaten that chicken sandwich from the galley. It had to be heartburn.

Once she cleared the worst of the snow and ice spots, I turned back to the door, where I typed in the code to get in. Agatha had given me all the codes years before. Opening the door, I set the suitcases down in the foyer.

Years before, a construction company had planned a line of these identical cabins along Sitka Lane, but after building the two at the end, the company went belly-up. The floor plans of the cabins were mirror images of each other. Agatha had bought this cabin with her late husband, Ernest, and my grandparents bought the opposite one. When they passed, they left it to me, their only grandchild.

"The kitchen is there, bathroom down the hall. The master bedroom is up the stairs in the loft. There's a side door that leads out to the hot tub and…"

"You really don't have to do all this. You're obviously not the owner of the house and don't have to help me." She glanced at the dark road between the two houses, worrying her lip between her teeth.

A rush of embarrassment ran through me. Of course she'd be worried about me knowing how to get into the house. She was a young woman, alone in a strange place, and I showed her I knew everything there was to getting around this house she was supposed to stay in. "If you're worried about anyone getting in, there's a strong deadbolt on the door. Lock it up tight once I leave, and no one can get in. Instructions for the alarm are in that binder." I pointed at the notebook on the coffee table.

She eyed the binder with trepidation. "Does this place have Wi-Fi or a landline phone? I need to call a tow truck for my car. And it doesn't seem like I have service."

So, that was her car on the street. I should have known. She seemed like the type to not know how to drive in the snow. Most people don't. The snowfall for the lowlands in Western Washington was middling at best, the cities decimated to a standstill with a few inches.

With my arms crossed against my chest, I frowned. "Of course that was you."

"Are you going to help me or make fun of me for my driving? Because I got to tell you, I feel dumb enough about this whole trip without you chiming in." She pulled off her beanie, tossing it to the counter. Her curly hair sprang loose around her face, little wisps of mahogany spirals and static. With her elbows on the kitchen counter, she ran her hands through her hair, covering her face.

"Service out here is pretty bad, but there should be Wi-Fi." I opened the binder and flipped through the pages. Glancing up, I saw her hand leave her forehead and come away with blood. "What happened?"

She blinked at me, frowning. "What? Oh, this?" She held up her hand. "I bumped my head on the steering wheel. It's not..."

Placing a hand on her shoulders, I pushed her down onto a stool and then pointed a finger at her. "Stay there. Do not move."

Finding the first aid kit took me a few tries, as Agatha didn't have it in any of the spots that made sense but instead in the pantry beside an expired box of dry tortellini. Returning to Wren, I was happy to see she hadn't moved, though she was typing on her phone and looking through the binder.

"Face me."

"You're bossy." She sulked but turned to face me, anyway. On the stool, she came up to my chin. Glancing down, I saw her feet were no longer on the ground.

"Look up." A swell of something swirled in my stomach as she followed my commands. Stepping between her legs, I peered down at her, looking at the injury and trying my damndest to ignore the soft heat coming from her body. At this angle, I could see the white bow of her bra between her breasts, but I wasn't going to look. Couldn't. Much.

Her skin was soft as I gently cleaned the scratch with a wipe. A sparking sensation traveled down my arm that I ignored as dried the area with a tissue. As gently as I could, I smoothed the bandage over the cut. Her jaw tensed, but she didn't make a sound. Once I was happy the bandage was on tight, I should have stepped back, but I didn't. My fingers moved from the spot on her hairline over to her temple. Her hairline was a riot of short loose curls, wild from her hat being removed. My hand twitched, wanting to touch one of those curls. Her eyes met mine, and I could have sworn I saw something dark behind her gaze that echoed my own feelings.

"Do you have a ringing in your ears, vomiting, confusion, headache?" I peered down at her, checking her pupils. Two warm amber eyes stared back at me, pupils of the same size.

"This whole day has been a headache," she grumbled. When I didn't ask for more, she shook her head. "No. Aside from the bump, I feel fine."

I didn't know this girl. Woman. Clearing my throat, I stepped out from between her legs.

I shouldn't be crowding her. Straightening, I crossed my arms against my chest and glanced around the room.

Why did I feel so responsible for this woman? I didn't know her. I had no ties to her. She was obviously capable of taking care of herself—but there was a funny tightening in my gut at the idea of her being here alone. "There's the wood stove there. Everything you need for a fire should be here."

"A wood fire?" she asked as she followed me to the stove. "Like matches and kindles?"

With a purse of my lips, I surveyed her. Okay, maybe not entirely capable. "Kindling, and yes."

With a furrow of her brow, she stared down at the cold stove. "Right. Can't be too hard. I've lit things on fire before."

I stood back, watching as she took a piece of wood in her hand, shoved it into the stove, lit a match, then dropped it onto the dry wood. The match burned down to the end and went out.

She lit another match—this time, holding it to the log. The fire burned down to her fingers, and she dropped it with a curse.

"Careful." I bent down beside her, taking her hand in mine to examine the burn. Her thumb had a small red spot. Turning her hand over inspected her further. No other damage.

"It's fine. I've burned my arm worse on a straightening iron." Her voice was soft as her eyes met mine.

I realized I had been holding her hand and dropped it quickly, standing up. "Could I—" I motioned to the fire. "I don't want to tell you what to do, but if you want help..."

"Please," she huffed out a relieved sigh. "I'm too cold and too tired for my pride to get in the way right now."

I waved for her to crouch beside me as I explained all the steps to building a good fire in this stove. She nodded along to my instruction, following them all until the fire caught on the newspaper and the log blackened. Her smile as she looked over at me stunned me. It was more than lips, teeth, and cheeks. It was an illumination. "Wow, I did that."

"Yeah." The breath in my lungs felt shaky as I tried to find the words. My tongue heavy at her smile. I cleared my throat. "It's easy enough if you learn how."

"I've never done that before. My parents have a pellet stove and then my apartment is all electric heat. There's no way a fire could be started by..." Her smile faded, and she glanced away, staring at the orange-and-white flames. "Anyway, thank you for teaching me."

"That's my job."

"Fire starter?"

I shook my head. "Teacher. High school English. Anyone can learn. You have to break it down into steps."

As I adjusted the logs over the kindling, she sucked in a breath. "Don't burn yourself."

"I've been building fires like this since I was in the single digits. Don't worry."

"I wasn't—I just..." She frowned. "I'm not used to being around someone who knows what they're doing."

I filed the odd comments away. She was a stranger. I didn't have a right to learn what that could mean.

"Right, I should get going. My dog must have heard my truck and is probably nervous that I haven't come in to feed her."

"Oh, you have a dog? What kind—no wait, let me guess. Golden retriever, German shepherd?"

"No, she's a..."

"A Burmese mountain dog. Or one of those big mastiff dogs?"

I coughed to hide my laugh at her exuberance. "She's definitely not any of those. Maizie is a mutt through and through. I couldn't even tell you her breed."

"But she's big, right? You look like the kind of guy who would have a big rough dog."

I pictured little wiry-haired Maizie. On her pile of special pillows, the hot pink quilt she had commandeered as her own lay beside her stash of small squeaky toys in her wicker basket beside her special formula kibble. "That's not how I would describe her."

"You should introduce me tomorrow." She opened the front door, leaning against it. Her hand on the door, she bit her lower lip and glanced between our two houses. The urge to pull her lip from her teeth came suddenly. Strike that down.

"Oh, um...maybe?" I stuttered for words. Was she asking to see me again? What was the right thing to say in this scenario? "I'll be over there if you need anything. And lock this deadbolt. No one or nothing is getting through it unless you want them to."

"Nothing? Not a ravenous bear?"

"No bears or nosy neighbors."

Her face softened, the flicker of a smile playing on those full lips. "The last thing I'd call you is nosy."

"What would you call me?" I wasn't sure where this bold question came from, but it came out before I could take it back.

"That remains to be seen." Her bright smile widened, dimples deepening on her cheeks. The sight of it was a gut punch. A heat pulsed through my chest. It didn't matter if I was standing on a snowy porch or if the wind was picking up, whipping shards of ice off the rail. I was all fire.

I needed to leave before I embarrassed myself in front of this beautiful woman. Clearing my throat, I motioned to the doorknob. "Lock this, Birdie."

If she had a reaction to the nickname, she didn't show it. She tapped the bandage on her forehead with two fingers. "Yes, sir."

At the base of the stairs, I paused, waiting for the telltale click of the deadbolt in the lock before traveling across the icy road to my home. Letting myself into the house, the wagging and nervous bundle of my dog greeted me, jumping up until her front paws were on my knees.

"I'm home, Maizie Girl. I'm home." Petting her coarse fur, I glanced at the house across the street, hoping to see one last glimpse of Wren.

Wren

DINNER WAS NAKED TORTELLINI, which turned out to be expired after I ate half of them, and a squished granola bar I fished out of the bottom of my suitcase. With a half-full belly, I fell asleep under three heavy blankets from the hall closet and woke up sweaty halfway through the night.

The fire Adrian and I made was still blazing in the wood stove, but I placed another log on the fire in case. My arms crossed over my chest, I stared at the flickering flames, heat warming my cheeks not from the fire but from embarrassment. The man likely thought I was a complete ninny. What kind of adult didn't know how to build a fire? What did he say he taught? High school? No wonder he was good at teaching me. He had experience with immature girls.

No. That wasn't fair. Sure, I wasn't a firestarter, but who even had a wood-burning stove these days? It's like crocheting a blanket instead of buying one at the store. I bet Adrian Winter couldn't make a killer charcuterie board for under thirty bucks.

Yeah, the circumstances of our meeting didn't paint me in the best light, but why would I care what this stranger thought of me? Even if he had intense blue-green eyes and callouses on his fingers that felt so good on my skin. And muscular arms that can lift a suitcase as if it was nothing and...

Nope, nope. Don't start daydreaming about the hunky man across the street.

A quick glance at my phone showed me I had one bar of service and seven unread messages, three from Buck. The towing company I called the night before said they'd have the dispatcher call me back in the morning.

Flopping onto the futon, I scanned the other messages I got. My friend Autumn sent daily affirmation she sent to our group text. Today's was *I trust that everything will be fine in due time.* Summer, my best friend, sent me a personal text, freaking out and asked for confirmation that I hadn't been eaten by a cougar or dumped in the woods by a serial killer. I ignored the affirmation—we all did—but let Summer know neither happened and that I managed to put my car into a snowbank. If the message even went through, it would be hours until she saw them. As I was about to put my phone down, my finger hovered over Buck's icon. The picture was one of him at the lake. We had spent the day on his parent's boat, him drinking heavily and me trying not to throw up from the seasickness as he made large wakes.

"You don't need to scream like that. I wasn't going that fast." Six months later, I could still feel the rising urge to ask him to let me off and the ultimate burying of my nausea. Staring at the picture now, it was as if it were a different man on that boat. That we were different people. The pictures I posted of that day are gold-beamed visions of a couple, carefree and in love. His nose slightly sunburned because "sunscreen is for losers" and my hair pulled free of my two braids. My sun hat was somewhere below the lake surface because he refused to go back and look for it.

Dozens of albums, I made on my phone, carefully organized for easy posting accessibility. Arranged by season, I'd post these pictures with cute sayings, tagging him.

Bile rose in my throat. All these pictures of us together. He would groan and complain before getting in them and flashing a breezy smile.

Three months I had been away from him, I kept waiting for the pain to come, but all I mourned was the loss of those years I had with him. The declined dates with the nice guy from my econ class junior year. The cute barista at my local coffee shop who would give me extra whipped cream. Countless girls' trips I had to decline because he would miss me if I went away. He certainly took his share of weekends with his boys. I told myself that everyone sacrifices for the people they love. We all make concessions. Only, I was the one hollowed out in the end.

One by one, I selected the pictures that were the worst lies. Him holding out the bouquet of grocery store discount flowers he only got me because he missed my mom's birthday dinner. Lounging on a pool float during our anniversary trip. The one where I spent most of the day holed up in the room sick with a stomach bug while he drank at the pool bar.

I stopped selecting them one by one and started deleting entire albums. Christmas gone. His cousin's wedding and the trip to see his favorite football team play. Cabo San Lucas gone.

Once I finished, I had only a quarter of my pictures left. Is this how much of my life was taken up by being with Buck? I left the pictures I liked of myself, especially the ones where my hair was natural. Buck preferred it when I straightened my hair, saying it was classier.

Fuck him.

Without reading his messages, I deleted the whole thread and then made the split-second decision to block his number on my phone. A sense of righteousness flowed through me. I should have done that years earlier. As I sank into the couch, I stared up at the wood ceiling, the swirls and circles of knots from century-old wood. Steady and strong. I could be that for myself.

Closing my eyes, I tried to imagine how I would spend my days on my own, relearning myself.

At some point in my sleep, I heard an engine but ignored it, rolling over and taking the blanket onto the floor with me. That's right, I fell asleep on the futon in front of the fire. Raising my head, I saw the fire was still burning.

With an audible groan, I pulled myself off the floor and trudged to the surprisingly spacious bathroom. My hair was—as it always was in the morning—wild. I had forgotten to put my bonnet on, and the curls were rebelling, as they always did. It took me over a year to wear my bonnet in front of Buck. He never said anything, but there was a definite pattern where he wouldn't want to have sex if I was wearing it.

Since the breakup, I had been back to wearing it every night, and my curls were all the better for it. Finger-combing the ringlets back, I braided them into a tight braid before washing the sleep from my eyes.

A large soaking tub sat in front of a window overlooking the trees and what must have been the Icicle Creek they named the town after. I might need to treat myself to a good soak when I got back from town.

Town. Drive. Car. Shit.

Grabbing my phone off the coffee table, I dialed the towing company.

The brisk woman on the other line informed me that their truck was currently running behind but that they could be out this afternoon to get my car. When she quoted me a price, I about dropped the phone.

Not that I was completely broke. My job as an analyst with Andra Data earned me enough to pay bills and the occasional trinket from Nordstrom. But the cost of this trip had already eaten into my savings enough that I might have to delay my move out of my parent's house for another month.

Straining my voice to sound as nonplussed as possible, I nodded as if she could see me through the phone. "Of course, not a problem."

"Please confirm the address for me."

"It's on Sitka La—"

"Oh, are you staying at Agatha's place? How is she? Don't tell me, somewhere warm. I've been meaning to visit her, but life got in the way."

"I'm not sure. I'm renting the place."

"Yes, yes, across from that Winter boy."

The last thing I would describe Adrian as was a boy. That man was all firm muscles and full lips and...

"Dammit," I cursed to myself.

"What was that?" the dispatcher asked.

Clenching my jaw, I took a deep inhale and tried to get the image of Adrian standing over me the night before out of my mind. The dip in my stomach as he walked out the door and ordered me to lock the door. The way those lips formed that little nickname, Birdie. Birdie. I had tried so hard not to react, but the space between my legs throbbed at the memory.

"Nothing." Walking to the front door, I pulled it open. Maybe a blast of cold air on my face would help. I stepped out onto the porch and stopped to stare at the car in front of me.

My car.

"Um, I'm sorry, ma'am. It appears I don't need towing after all."

I gave my goodbye, letting my hand fall to my side.

How did he do that? Still, in my thick socks, I walked down the recently shoveled stairs and peered closer.

Yep, my car, the same little dent on the hood from where my younger brother's basketball hoop fell on it. I even spied the crushed bag of chips on the passenger seat.

"How..." My knowledge of unsticking cars from snowbanks was minimal, but there was no way it would be easy.

Digging my buzzing phone out of my coat pocket, I considered if I even wanted to see the screen, knowing it might be Buck asking for yet another thing. Then I remembered I blocked him the night before.

Answering quickly, I barely got out a *hello* before my best friend Summer was bellowing in my ear.

"Wren Louise Alexander, what the hell do you think you're doing, leaving in the middle of the night?"

"That's not my middle name, and I left town at one in the afternoon yesterday. It's not my fault you don't check your phone."

Summer made a displeased sound on the other end. "So, I'm guessing you didn't get eaten by a bear or let any other terrible fate befall you."

"Well..." I cringed. "About that. I may have accidentally—very much not on purpose—put my car into a snowbank after trying to take a turn too quickly."

"Wren!"

"Shouldn't you be on a plane? Why are you calling me?"

"My dad is driving me in thirty. I already said goodbye to Cory." I could picture her in her small apartment, packing her multiple oversized suitcases. She was set to travel to London for a hotelier management internship for some fancy company. "You're changing the subject. Do I need to rally the troops to rescue you?"

"It's already been freed. The neighbor across the street pulled it out this morning with his truck."

Even over the phone and over a hundred miles from my best friend, I could sense the cogs in her mind whirring as she quizzed me on the neighbor.

He seems like he's in his late twenties.

I don't know if he's single.

His name is Adrian Winter.

Yeah, okay, I'll admit he is extremely attractive.

Content with my answers, I could practically hear the smile on her face as she said, "If he seems okay, you should sleep with him."

The thought had been playing in a perpetual loop in my head, but to do it was wild. "I barely know the man. Besides, after embarrassing myself twice in front of him, I'm sure the last thing he would want is me throwing myself at him."

"Men don't pull a woman's car out of the ditch unless they want something."

"Nice men do."

"Nice men? When have you ever dated a nice man?" Summer asked with humor in her words.

I frowned at the comment. She wasn't wrong, but jeez.

"Harsh."

"But true," she reminded me. "Are you going to sit here now and tell me that *Buck* was a nice boyfriend? No way. You have a type, and they are not kind men. I get the appeal in theory. A bad boy can be fun, but after the honeymoon wears off, he's just an asshole."

"Okay, I get it. I have bad taste." I wasn't going to mention that the guy she was dating refused to meet us. Sure, I might have a bad boy or two under my belt, but at least the men I dated would show up.

"Let your bad taste run for one more time and try to find someone to hook up with in that town. It's by the resort. I bet there'll be all sorts of hot skiers in the lounge that would take you back to their chalet," she said chalet with an accent.

The idea of sitting at some resort bar waiting for a pink-cheeked man drunk on ten-dollar IPAs to flirt with me made my stomach roll. Despite what Summer thought, I didn't set out to find an asshole boyfriend. They found me. And really, it was only two in all my dating history. Three, if you counted the two dates I had with the guy who drove an old Camaro and hung out in the grocery store parking lot—though that guy had the best hair I had ever seen on a man. "Hanging up now. I love you. A bear has not eaten me."

Before Summer could give me any more unwelcome advice, I shoved my phone in my coat pocket and headed out the door. In the morning light, I could see a pathway between the two houses, from one freshly shoveled set of stairs to the other.

Passing his large white truck, I stood on my tiptoes to peek into the window. Black sunglasses clipped on the sun visor and a travel coffee tumbler in the cupholder. No napkins, no squashed chip bags or crumbled receipts.

On the porch, my fist hovered over the door. Should I knock? Was it too early? He had already gotten my car out of the ditch, so he was obviously up at one point, but maybe he went back to bed? Before I lost my nerve, I knocked twice, stepping back and wrapping my arms around my body.

I heard the soft sound of footsteps and a high-pitched clicking noise.

Adrian opened the door, wearing a dark-blue Henley and gray sweatpants. My eyes darted to the front of his pants briefly before snapping to his face. Was that a shadow, or was he packing down there?

"I..." I was rarely at a loss for words, but damn if this man didn't look better in the daylight.

Something that resembled a dirty brown mop launched itself at my knees, little dark eyes staring up at me and pink tongue lolling out to the side.

"Maizie, stop it." Adrian grabbed the dog—that's what that thing must have been—and picked it up to cradle in his arms.

The dog watched me, her little paws resting on Adrian's muscular chest. His shirt was slightly unbuttoned, and I glimpsed a swath of his collarbone. How could a collarbone be sexy? I had been reading too many Regency romances if an exposed neck was doing things for me.

"Sorry, we don't get company often, and she loves new people."

"That's okay." I reached forward and gave the dog a scratch behind her ear. She rewarded me with a lick of my hand.

"She likes you."

"I like her. Maizie, you said?" Moving from her ear to her chin, I realized I was closer to him now.

"Maizie, the lazy girl. A tourist I brought back to my old apartment left her behind but took all my silverware."

Tourist. He said it casually, as if he had tourists in his home—*in his bed, more likely*—all the time. "Wow, sorry." The admission surprised me.

"We're better for it. Maizie here is worth more than a bunch of old spoons."

Clearing my throat, I motioned to my car behind me. "Thank you. I'm assuming you're responsible for the emancipation of my car."

"Luckily, you left your keys in. I stuck it in neutral."

"Oh, right. Oops." Warmth colored my cheeks as I added forgotten keys to the list of foolish things I had accomplished in the twelve hours since meeting this man. "Anyway, that was really kind."

He swallowed, his eyes glancing from the car to my face. "It's not a big deal. Only took a few minutes."

Stepping closer, I slapped a hand on my chest. "No, but it is. I called the towing company, and they were quoting me three hundred dollars to come up here. I do not have that kind of money."

"Who does?" He gave me a small smirk. It was barely a smile, but something in my stomach did flip at the sight.

I fought against answering *my stupid ex does*. Instead, I motioned to the car. "I don't know how you did it without me hearing it."

"I use a winch."

"A wench?" I asked, my brow furrowing. "Like old-timey barmaids from pirate romances?"

His words slow, he blinked a few times. "No. I don't think we're talking about the same thing."

"You know, bar wench—'Bring me some ale, wench!'" I mimicked doing a motion similar to a drunken pirate cheering with a tankard.

"Definitely not." His face was serious, but I saw a glimmer of humor in his eyes as if he were trying to hold back a laugh.

As if my face could get any hotter from embarrassment.

"Regardless, I'd like to thank you. I have to go into town to get some groceries. Could I buy you lunch?"

He motioned me in. Once we got inside, I saw his hair wasn't as dark as I thought, more of a warm golden than brown. But his eyes were still an intense shade of blue green.

Once, as a child, I was dock fishing with my dad when a storm rolled through, bringing black-gray clouds and biting wind. We could see the rain was coming toward us, darkening everything. It was a few minutes of torrential downpour on top of us and then the rain let up. The clouds parted, and the sea below was a squall of blue green.

I motioned to the picture on the wall of a couple standing in front of a glittery backdrop. The older woman in a gold gown with her white hair styled in sprayed curls and an older man in an ill-fitting suit. Both of them beaming at each other, the deep wrinkles around their eyes and mouths showing years of laughter and a life well lived. "Are these your grandparents?"

Adrian smiled at the picture, a softness in his eyes. "Yeah, about two years ago. They went on one of those European river cruises—the Danube and the Reine. My gran had three glasses of Riesling at one spot and called me at five a.m. to tell me I was a good grandson."

The tenderness in his gaze gave me a funny tumbling in my stomach. "It looks like they're having a great time. I wish I could do something like that, but I'd probably throw up the whole time." Glancing over at him, I ducked my head. "Seasickness. I'm fine in other places—cars and airplanes—but something about being on the water makes me nauseated."

"I won't buy that boat, then."

"You can, but I won't get on it." The simple statement was out of my mouth before I thought about it. How many times did I suffer on a trip with Buck, dosed up with antiemetics and hoping for the best because he insisted that "this time, it wouldn't be so bad," only to find myself barfing over the edge while he shotgunned a light beer?

"Nah, things like that are only fun as long as everyone is having a good time. I'll save my money."

There is no future here. It's just flirtation. It's not a sign of anything.

I motioned back to the picture. "Your grandparents sound great. You have your grandpa's smile."

The mirror image reflected at me, the same little curve of his lip, the way his cheeks stretched wide for his grin. "No one's ever told me that before. Thank you. Everyone said he had the greatest smile."

Before I second guess myself, I blurted out, "I think your smile is pretty great."

His cheeks colored slightly at the comment, and he snorted as he turned away. "All right, um. Let me change, and we can get going."

Cursing myself for telling him that, I glanced around the room. The layout of his space was a mirror of the cabin across the street. Inside, I could see little things glancing through the window had blocked. His flannels and jackets were still hanging up on the wall, a row of shoes below. Strewn over the side of the couch was a hot pink pillow with a basket of fuzzy toys beside it. Maizie ambled up to the pillow, turned three times, and then plopped down. Her large brown eyes were on me as I took in the room.

I heard footsteps above me as Adrian dressed. Since the homes were identical, I knew that if I moved slightly to the left, I could see up into his room. Glancing over at the dog, I swear she gave me a head shake that said, *are you really about to do this?*

"No snitching," I whispered to the dog. She blinked at me a few times before putting her head down. I took that as acceptance.

As stealthy as I could be, I tiptoed into the kitchen, craning my neck to see up the wooden stairs and into the loft bedroom. His back to me, Adrian pulled his shirt over his head. His trapezoid muscles rippled as he moved toward the closet. He truly was a specimen. Sure, I had seen shirtless men plenty of times over the years, but the last I was alone with was Buck. Two of Buck's forearms would be the same size as one of Adrian's. Not to mention, Buck's waist didn't have those adorable little dimples right over his ass. Unbidden, I imagined how my thumbs would fit there as he thrust inside me.

I was never much for daydreaming about sex, but the thoughts this man giving me. This Adrian Winter was a different man indeed.

Standing in front of his dresser, he pulled out a shirt and a pair of jeans. With rapt attention that I knew was wrong, I watched as his thumbs hooked into the waistband of his sweatpants, pulling them down and kicking them to the side. My mouth dropped open as I took in the scene before me. He wasn't wearing underwear. His bare ass on display. And what an ass it was. Shapely and firm, if I had daydreamed about my hands on his body before, this took it up to a level three thousand.

This was crossing a line. Shirtless was one thing, but to watch him completely naked and not look away, I had to be crossing a line.

Look away.

Anytime now, look away.

I couldn't. How was a man so graceful when getting dressed? He stepped out of view for a moment, returning with boxer briefs and unbuttoned jeans. A small sigh escaped my lips. His back still facing me, I memorized the planes of his muscles as he pulled the long-sleeved shirt over his head. My tongue came out to wet my lips, and my breath was heavy.

His hands on the front of his jeans, he glanced over his shoulder and stopped. His eyes locked on mine, and I knew I should look away, appear casual. Be anything but a creeper, but instead, I froze.

While I had little experience with being caught watching a man dress, his calmness surprised me.

"How long have you been standing there?" he asked, a brow quirked. Slow as a panther stalking its prey, he walked down the stairs, his gaze never leaving my face.

"I...um." Now would have been a great time to be sexy or flirtatious or *something.* But instead, I glanced over at the dog and blurted, "She seemed thirsty, so I was going to fill her water bowl. That's why I'm standing here."

Maizie blinked up at me with an expression of, *don't bring me into your little peeping kink.*

Adrian stepped down on the landing, his eyes darting to the dog, who was now lying on her back, her feet up in the air and making low snuffling noises. "Is that so?"

"Uh." I hesitated. "Yes?"

He sauntered closer until his body was practically against mine. Warmth radiated from him. I leaned back against the counter, my hands gripping the edge for stability. Leaning down, his face inches from mine, a small smile tugging at his full lips. "You're a terrible liar."

This was dangerous. My body betrayed me as I let out another sigh. His skin smelled of cedar and faint smoke. A natural scent of cutting his own wood and making his own fire. Nothing like the expensive cologne I was used to.

"See anything you like?"

"No," my voice was shaky.

This time, his words were hot on my ear. "You shouldn't lie, *Birdie.*"

Oh, what that phrase was doing for me.

His nose brushed against my hair, and I heard the distinct sound of him inhaling against me. The pulsing between my thighs became an ache. I clamped my legs together and gripped the counter tighter.

Straightening up, he nodded his head in the opposite direction. "The dog bowl is in the bathroom. She'll be fine for the day. Should we go?"

The smirk on his face told me he was well aware of what his presence was doing to me.

I nodded, following him out the door on jelly legs. On the bottom step leading to the car, I stumbled slightly on a loose stone under the snow. His hand came out, grabbing hold of my arm and catching me before I fell on my butt. How could I possibly embarrass myself more?

"Oops." Even through my thick jacket, I could feel the strength of his grip on me, holding me steady. My eyes came up to his. Seriously, how were they such a color?

"We're in no rush. Take your time."

Pursing my lips, I pulled my arm out of his grip. My body may tell me to make terrible decisions, but in the crisp air, I could get more clarity. I wasn't some hormonal fool, and I could walk without assistance.

One step at a time, I made my way down the shoveled walkway, heading toward my car.

"Where are you going?" he asked behind me.

"My car." I motioned to my somewhat trusty silver vehicle.

"No. I'm driving."

My arms crossed against my chest, I frowned. "I can drive."

Without responding, he glanced from my car to the other end of the street, where my car had been pulled out of a snowbank.

"I'll have you know that is the first accident I've been in. If you can even call that an accident."

"It's a bad idea is what it is. Get in the truck."

Pride and sense warred inside me. I knew the likelihood of me getting into town in my car was fairly good. But was it great? No. But did I want to be bossed around by this man?

Okay, yeah, maybe a bit. Sense, and my libido won out.

One hand on the passenger side door, his other hand held out to boost me up into the seat. His palm had calluses, workingman's hands. Buck's hands were softer than mine. As I put my hand in his, a warmth shot up my arm. A tingly sensation flooded through me.

As much as I wanted to fight the feeling, I liked the rasp of my palm against his. It was only a moment of contact, but as he shut my door and walked to the driver's side, I ran a finger over my love line to get the sensation to stay. My mother told me once that my love line was long but my head line was broken. That I had the capacity to love deeply but that love would take over logic and reason. To be careful who I trusted my heart with. Palm reading never seemed like something I could believe in, but in that moment, her words rang true.

"There's a water bottle in the door if you get thirsty." He motioned to the cup holder.

"You keep water bottles in your car?" I asked, pulling out the bottle. "You get a lot of thirsty women in your car?"

His cheeks turned pink as he spared a quick glance at me. "No, Birdie."

Heat pulsed through me at the name. I crossed my legs at the sensation. It was a silly nickname. Why was it so hot? Swallowing down all the questions I had, I glanced out the window at the snow lined trees.

CHAPTER FOUR

Adrian

L AST NIGHT, AFTER KNOWING she was safe behind the deadbolt, I went straight into the shower and tried washing my day on the slope off me. My mind was less on the grime of sweat and more on the look in her eyes as I put that bandage on her head. The fullness of those lips begging to be kissed long and hard. My hand drifted down to my hard cock, and it only took a few minutes before I was spending all over the shower wall, my hand braced against the cold tile for support. I barely touched her, didn't know her at all, and she was already responsible for the most intense jerk-off session I've ever had.

I've never been one for preternatural senses, but as I took my shirt off at the house, I felt her eyes on me. There was no reason she would stand in the spot she was in, and I certainly wasn't rushing through getting dressed. I could see the reflection of her standing there in my mirror, the angle wonky enough so that she wouldn't realize that I could see her. So, yeah, I put on a show. At first, it was just my shirt being off and then it was everything. Don't peep into someone's bedroom while they're changing unless you want a show.

And the way she stammered and flushed as I called her out. Not going to lie, it made my dick hard. Would her skin flush that same color if I touched her?

The ride down the mountain only took fifteen minutes, and her face was turned away the whole time, watching out the window. I hoped I hadn't scared her away when I stood close to her. Did I come off a little strong? Yeah. But something more than myself spurned me on. I had my share of women I've flirted with. But I never invaded their space, cornering them against a counter and sniffing them.

And her scent. She smelled of warmth and apples somehow. I wanted to bottle that scent and carry it with me. Desperately, I wanted it splayed on my pillows, and, yes—I wanted to breathe her in as I sunk into her.

That scent was now filling up the cab of my truck. I didn't want to open the door and have it escape.

Walking the aisles of the grocery store, I pushed the cart behind Wren as she stopped every few feet to grab something and toss it into the cart. She used no list and there didn't seem to be a rationale for her items. From my position, I could watch as she moved. Her shirt riding up to expose a swath of smooth bronze skin, the way her jeans fit her ass. It was a great ass, round and soft. The perfect size for cupping as I thrust inside her.

I had to adjust my growing erection in the pasta and beans aisle. She turned to me, two different pasta sauces in her hands. Quickly, I thought of boner killers: my mom's corned beef dinners and the sight of my high school English teacher when he sneezed and his fake tooth came out. That seemed to do the trick.

"What do you think? Cheap sauce or the ten-dollar organic stuff?"

I cleared my throat, staring at the sauces for a bit too long. "Um, organic?"

She nodded as if that was what she wanted me to say. In the wine and beer aisle, she studied the bottles before moving down to the end and grabbing a few clearance cans of wine off an end rack.

At the cookie aisle, she clapped her hands together. "They have my favorite!" She turned around to show me a bag of gourmet wafers and dark chocolate. "These are so hard to find, and they are the best thing ever."

Taking them from her hand, I studied them. "No way those are the best"—I grabbed another package off the shelf—"when you can have these."

She scoffed at me. "You're kidding, right? You must have burned off taste buds if you think there is a cookie better than my beloved."

I threw both packages in the cart. "Fine, we'll do a blind taste test, and from there, the winner will be determined."

"How do I know you won't cheat?" she asked.

Narrowing my eyes at her, I pretended to pull out a sword. "Are you besmirching my honor? We duel at dawn."

She laughed a bright, wonderful thing that made my stomach do a little flip.

"What do I get if I win?"

A kiss.

I swallowed that idea down. "How about if I win, you have to admit I have superior taste in grocery brand cookies and buy me a bag of my favorite?"

"And if you lose?"

I smirked at her. "What do you want?"

Her eyes flickered to my mouth before darting back up to my eyes. "You need to buy me three bags of cookies."

Sticking my hand out, I waited for her to take it. "Deal."

As she took my hand, a sizzle traveled up my arm and into my chest. Her palm was warm and soft, fitting perfectly in mine. The pad of my thumb brushed softly over the back of her hand. I had the impulse to lace my fingers with hers, right here in the middle of this grocery store. She looked up at me, her eyes a warm topaz.

The rattle of another grocery cart had us springing apart. Wren cleared her throat, her hand rubbing at a spot behind her left ear. Her gaze looking everywhere but me, she walked on, with me pulling up the rear.

The cart was half full as she led me down the cleaning aisle.

"The cabin supplies are atrocious." She grabbed several items, her arms full of cans and bottles.

"I'm sure if you let Agatha know she'll have the cleaners come back."

Dumping them in the cart, Wren blew a curl away from her face. "It's fine for other people, but I need like *clean* clean. I used up pretty much all her stuff under the sink last night."

"You? Need clean?" When I was moving her car earlier, I noticed the various pieces of clutter around her car, a chip bag, napkins, and receipts stuck in the side cup holder.

"You really going to judge me on how my car looks at the moment of an accident? I obviously couldn't carry all the garbage and my suitcase at the same time. Plus, everyone knows there's a difference between a woman's car and her home. I enjoy cleaning. It soothes me."

I put my hands up in defeat. "Okay, message received."

At the other end of the aisle, I saw a man and turned my body away from them, ducking to the endcap display of candles, flashlights, and batteries. Squeezing myself against the display, I glanced over at Wren, who was watching me with a bemused expression.

"You good?"

I shook my head, my voice low. "Let me know when that guy is gone."

Her eyes darted down the aisle. "Umm, I don't think—"

"Mr. Winter, is that you?" The man sidestepped Wren and her cart to stand in front of me.

"Hello, Mr. Nilson. How's midwinter break treating you?" I straightened up. No point in running now.

"Good, good." The man shoved his hands in his pockets and leaned closer. "Though I'm still waiting to hear about that test, Christopher failed. Now, from what I understand, there were study guides that he never received, and I think because of that, he should be able to retake the test."

I sighed. "As I told your wife last week, Christopher had access to the study guide in the online classroom. He had the same chance to access as every other child in the class. In fact, I checked before responding to your wife, and Christopher did click on the study guide three times but never for longer than five minutes. He also spent a large part of time in my class playing King of Kingdoms instead of completing the practice test."

The man's face turned puce colored, and he straightened up, so he was now at my chin. "Now see here. My tax dollars are paying for you to teach my son. I will take your response to the principal."

Sighing, I rubbed a hand over my face. "That's your right to do. Her email is the first letter of her name and then her last name."

He glared at me, then at Wren for good measure before hustling down the dog food aisle.

Wren was biting her lip, as if concerned. "You okay?"

"Yeah. Small-town teacher stuff. Nothing I haven't dealt with before." Grabbing the cart, I pulled it toward me. "You ready?"

She nodded, following me as I pushed the cart to the checkout.

Her groceries packed carefully in the bed of my truck and under the canopy bed protector, I was holding the door open to my favorite diner outside the city limits. It was a local favorite, but its distance from the touristy downtown area made it harder for out-of-towners to try.

She glanced around, taking in the kitschy decor.

Hesitating at the door, I stared down at her. Those silly white boots on her feet and an expensive jacket. She probably wanted a place with a prix fixe menu and white tablecloths. "Is this place okay? I can take you somewhere nice."

"No, this place is adorable. I love it. I am surprised you wanted to come here." She motioned to the quilt on the wall and the framed doilies. Her warm amber eyes lit up with humor.

"I love this place. They have the best burgers here. And—"

"Adrian Winter, where have you been hiding out?" a sharp voice barked from a back room. Marta Hunt, the owner, came out. Wearing a tee shirt that said, *Those who think they know it all are really annoying to those of us who do.* A pink apron tied around her waist, and her silver hair pulled back in a low ponytail. Her shrewd dark-brown eyes glanced from me to Wren.

After a quick hug, I motioned to Wren. "Mrs. Hunt, this is Wren Alexander. She is renting Agatha's cabin for the next week."

The slender woman looked at Wren appraisingly and hummed under her breath before looking back at me. I could see the words in her gaze. *What are you bringing her in here for?*

I realized from that gaze that I had never brought a date to this place. If that's what being with Wren could be called. She had said it was a thank-you for pulling her car out, but there was no way I was going to let her treat me. Any good Samaritan would have done the same thing. Too late now.

"Mrs. Hunt was good friends with my grandparents."

"God rest their souls." She turned to Wren, a small smile on her face. "I was very close with Gerald and Winifred for years. Even though he was my beau first. But we all knew there was no fighting against a true love like theirs."

"They sound like great people."

A pang of hurt rippled out of my chest. Losing grandparents wasn't a unique experience, but somehow, hearing those words with Wren by my side made the sensation all the more acute. "They were."

Mrs. Hunt motioned to a table in the back with a small vase of plastic flowers on it.

As we approached, I pulled out the chair for Wren. She glanced up at me with those warm eyes. Like whiskey on the rocks burning down my chest. Her normally smiling mouth made a small O, and her brows wrinkled.

She mumbled a thanks as she settled in. Once I was across from her, I looked down at the menu taped under the clear glass top. I knew what I was getting. I always got the same thing, but the warmth of Wren's gaze on me was too much.

Why would it be such a surprise to her when I held the chair out for her? From an early age, my grandfather instilled that in me. Now, doing those motions felt like an homage to him.

Mrs. Hunt came to the table, her eyes on Wren. "I know what this one is getting, but what would you like?"

Wren's left hand rested on the side of her face as she glanced down at the menu, ordering a cheeseburger with a fried egg on top. Which was my exact order.

Mrs. Hunt glanced at me, a smile quirking on the corner of her mouth. "Right away."

Wren glanced at the framed pictures on the wall, awards for the best burger in Icicle Creek five years before. T-ball team photos and fundraisers for high school boosters.

"You never told me what brought you up here."

Frowning, she took a small sip of her soda.

"You don't have to if it's too personal."

She shook her head. "It's not that it's too personal. It's more embarrassing. My boyfriend—well, ex now—had me plan this trip for my birthday. But we broke up, and I forgot to cancel the reservation. It was nonrefundable and on my credit card, so I figured I might as well use it."

"Wait, you planned your own birthday trip?" This guy sounded like an asshole.

She nodded at me before glancing away, pink coloring her cheeks. Her fingers rubbed behind her left ear. "It was easier that way. I didn't mind."

"Bullshit."

She blinked at me, her brown eyes large. "What?"

"Bullshit you didn't mind. No one should have to plan their own birthday trip, let alone pay for it."

At this time, Mrs. Hunt came to the table, dropping off our identical plates, leaving me with a look of warning I took to mean *don't screw this up*. I waited until Wren took a big bite of her burger before asking, "Why would you be embarrassed by that?"

Her eyes met mine, and her chewing slowed. I waited as she took a big drink of her soda before she answered wistfully. "I know it all makes me sound pathetic."

"He's the pathetic one. It should embarrass him for being such a little bitch when he had a girl like you."

"You don't even know me." Her voice was soft, but a brief flicker of something hard flashed behind her eyes. She liked what I said.

"I know enough." Sitting back in my chair, I surveyed her. I wasn't sure when the last time I truly noticed a woman. But with Wren, I wanted to know everything.

Giving me a halfhearted smile, she sat back, her eyes leaving mine. There was a long silence between us, and I wondered if I had freaked her out. This time, her voice was harder as she stared out the window behind me. "Buck always said he'd take me up to the mountains, but he never did."

"Buck? Your ex-boyfriend's name is Buck?"

She nodded, shrugging. "Yeah, so?"

"Buck is a verb. It's not a name."

Wren wrinkled her nose. "Buck is a nickname. Beaufort Terrence Rebel Lark the Fourth is his full name."

There was a long silence where I blinked at her, my mouth opening and closing with unspoken words. "I...Okay, that is so much worse."

"It's a family name."

"It's dumb." I tapped a finger on my lips. "He sounds like a Confederate soldier. And that last name is even worse. Bird, bird."

She pulled her lower lips in between her teeth as she stared at my mouth. Did I have ketchup on it? I grabbed a napkin, wiping myself quickly. She blinked a few times as if breaking from a trance. "Huh?"

A crease formed between my thick brows. "Lark. If you took his last name, your name would have been Wren Lark."

She took a fry, chewing slowly as she came up with her answer. "Yeah..."

"...And I'm going to take a wild guess since he is the unfortunate fourth man in his family to have that name that he isn't a fan of women keeping their names."

"I guess it's a good thing it didn't work out," she stated plainly before taking the last bite of her burger. Pushing her plate away, she stood up from the table. "I'll be right back."

Mrs. Hunt came back, placing the check on my side of the table. Good gal. I slipped my credit card into the slot.

"Glad to see you're not going to let her pay."

I was already planning on it, but now, I had no choice. "Of course not."

"She's a lovely girl."

"She is." I agreed.

"You want to tell me what's going on there?"

"You're too nosy. I barely know her. It was just lunch."

"And yet you bring her here. Your favorite restaurant in town, with your favorite person."

"Bull. Who says you're my favorite person?"

"Don't get cheeky. If this girl was nothing to you, you would have taken her downtown to one of those revolving restaurants that serve bratwurst and tankards of beer. Not bring her to meet me."

"Maybe I was craving your burgers."

Mrs. Hunt raised a brow at me. "Now who's full of shit?"

Wren emerged from the bathroom, fresh red lipstick on, her hair smoother than before. I wanted to smudge that lipstick and muss her hair.

"Wren. It was lovely to meet you. Make sure you come back to see me again. You don't need to bring this guy around."

"Hey!" I protested.

"I'd love to, Mrs. Hunt," Wren said as she sat back down across from me.

She laid a hand on top of Wren's. "Please call me Marta."

She never offered for me to call her by her given name.

"Marta." Wren smiled up at the woman.

"Winnie would have liked you," Mrs. Hunt said.

Wren's cheeks colored slightly at the comment, her finger rubbing behind her left ear, but she smiled at the older woman.

"You've said two words to her," I grumbled. Not that I disagreed with her, but did she have to show such preferential treatment?

Mrs. Hunt glared at me. "I know what I know, boy."

As I shook my head, I opened the holder, signing my name to the credit card receipt.

"Hey, I was supposed to pay that." She reached forward, her hands trying to grab the case from me.

Holding it out of her reach, Mrs. Hunt swooped by, grabbing it. "I already paid. Let me take care of you."

A flash of something—shock, maybe—flashed in her eyes before she sat back. "You mean the check?"

Swallowing, I thought back to my words. Did I mean the check? I should have said it, not you. But I couldn't bring myself to take back the sentiment. I wanted to take care of this woman. I never had that urge before. "Of course, the check."

Pursing her lips, she studied me. "Can I at least buy you a drink? There had to be a bar around here, right? For those thirsty tourists you seem to love."

I frowned at her comment. Was it spot on? Obviously. But coming from her, I didn't like it. "There are a few wine bars and beer halls."

"No real bar?"

"There's The Horse and Trails, but it's a dive. Astroturf carpet and windows that steam up when more than ten people are inside."

"Perfect. I love dive bars. The grimier, the better."

I glanced down at her perfect red polished nails that matched her red lipstick. "Really?"

"You think I can't slum it? I can."

Wren

I COULDN'T STOP STARING at his lips. The entire time we were at the diner, I watched as he ate his food, the way his lips touched the glass of his soda—the form and shape of his mouth as he spoke. I was watching his lips so much I missed half of what he said. Until he brought up the terrible last name I escaped from. After graduation, quite a few of our friends got engaged. One by one, I saw the pattern. While twenty-four was too young for me to marry, enough of our friends joked about "our turn." Worst of all, it didn't escape my notice that, if they did, what my name would be.

Buck and I talked about marriage exactly one time. It was more him ranting for twenty minutes after his cousin's wedding. He would never allow his fiancée to do anything as gauche as giving herself away. I held my tongue.

But Adrian was right: Buck was a traditionalist. That he would marry someone and allow them to keep their last name was as preposterous as owning a car over five years old.

On the walk to the bar, I took my place on the roadside of the sidewalk. Adrian set his hand on my shoulder and gently steered me to the side until he was between me and the road. Even through my long-sleeved shirt and oversized jacket, I could feel the warmth of his touch going straight into the center of me. I wrapped my arms around my chest, trying to keep the sensation in. I pulled my gloves out of my coat pocket and pulled them on. They were still damp from when I slipped the day before.

Adrian frowned at my hands. "Are those wet?"

I shrugged. "Not too bad. Better than nothing."

He shook his head, grabbing one of my hands with his bare fingers. The warmth of his skin leeched through my wet gloves. A tingle traveled up my arm at the contact. "You can't wear these gloves. They're soaked through. You're going to lose a finger like that."

He grasped the finger of my glove, pulling it off each finger one by one. There was something deeply erotic about the way his hands moved over mine, exposing my skin. Every brush of his fingers sent waves up my arm and straight down my body to my center. There was no way he could know what this action was doing to me. He was taking off my gloves, not my bra. Why was it so hot?

With the damp gloves shoved into his coat pocket, he took both my hands between his and rubbed them. "Is that better? Are you cold?" he asked, his ocean eyes scanning me. "Do you want me to get my flannel out of the car?"

With a smile, I pulled my hands away, shoving them in my pocket. I didn't need to swoon over his sense of chivalry. "No, I'm fine. It's only a few blocks, right?"

He stopped in front of a wooden door with chipped paint that read, *T e Hor e and T ails*. "It's here, but I can still run back to the truck if you're too cold."

"Absolutely not. I'm fine." I reached forward to grab the door handle, and he got there first, opening the door for me. In the doorway, I stopped under him. His arm flexed above me. The tendons on the back of his hand tensed. I could make out the smattering of light freckles in the low light.

Strong hands, capable. The memory of my palm against his as I climbed down from his truck, the brush of his fingers on my forehead the night before. I blinked up at him, trying to get my musings in check.

The bar smelled slightly of old beer, dust, and grease. A wood-burning stove was in the corner, and small heaters were arranged around the green carpet floor. A young woman was behind the bar, wearing a sweatshirt that said, *The Horse and Trails Pub, worst service in twenty miles.*

"Hey, Jordan." Adrian waved at her before motioning to me to order.

I glanced over at the drink specials on the neon dry-erase board, ordering the beer on special. The heat from the stove made the air feel stuffy, but the cold air from the opening door mingled together.

The bartender set two beers down in front of us, and Adrian held out his card.

"Absolutely not." I pushed his hand away, savoring the tingles that shot up my arm at the contact. "I said I would pay. It's a cheap beer. I can cover it."

Adrian made a face but shoved his card back in his wallet with a frown. "You're impossible—you know that?" he asked.

"Me? How about you?" I shot back.

"How am I impossible, Birdie?"

The bartender glanced between me and Adrian, a smirk on her face. "I like this one."

"No one asked you, Jordan." Adrian scowled, shaking his head good-naturedly.

The bartender laughed at him, turning her back to the register.

I lean forward, knowing that I have the bartender's approval. "Hey, do you like cookies?"

Jordan turned back to face me. "Sure, who doesn't?"

"Don't..." Adrian started, but I already had the two different bags of cookies out of my purse. "How did you fit them in there?"

I shot a warning glare at Adrian. "A girl's purse is full of mysteries." Turning back to Jordan, I set one cookie from each package on a napkin. "Taste these and tell us which one is better."

"You don't have to." Adrian made a move to take the cookies away, and Jordan batted his hand.

"Get off my cookies, you fiend." She picked up the first one, taking a nibble on the edge, then tilted her head to the side and swallowed. "A little crumbly, but the chocolate is smooth and thick."

Picking up the other cookie, she took a bigger bite. "Now, this one has a denser cookie, but the chocolate is a little too thin." She popped the rest of the cookie in her mouth, then added the other.

I leaned in closer. "Well, which one is better?"

Taking her time chewing, she cocked her head to the side. By the time she swallowed, we leaned forward, our eyes on her. In my peripheral vision, I saw Adrian motioning to himself and mouthing to Jordan.

"No cheating!" I scowled at him.

Putting his hands up in mock surrender, he adopted an innocent expression. "I wasn't cheating. I was only reminding her who brought her a can of gas a few years ago when she ran out on the side of the road."

My stool swiveling to the right, I poked a finger into his arm. "No. None of that. This is a clear cookie-tasting competition, and if you say another word, you'll forfeit to me. Remember, duel's at dawn."

With wide eyes on the other side of the bar, Jordan covered her mouth to hide her smile. "Like I said, I like this one."

"Pick your damn cookie, Jordan," he grumbled.

Jordan pondered the choices, asking for two more of each before she could make her final choice, finally landing on his cookie. I admitted defeat with as much class as I could muster, acknowledging that he had the superior taste in cookies. The smile he gave me made my ribs too tight, and I had to glance away.

We grabbed our drinks off the faded bar top and turned away. "Come on." With his free hand, Adrian touched the small of my back. Leading me away from the bar and to a small round table in the corner. A heater sat a few feet away, warm air blowing toward us. Adrian set his beer down on the table and grabbed the back of the peeling pleather chair to pull it out for me.

"I can pull out my own chair, you know," I remarked as I sat down.

"But why should you?" He sat across from me, taking a long drink. His eyes on me as I tried to come up with an answer.

It wasn't as if I had never had my chair pulled out or doors opened for me. What I wasn't used to was his effortless way of it. I didn't get the sense this was because he wanted something from me or was trying to impress me. It was his natural inclination.

To admit how foreign the act was to me felt too raw. I had already told him about Buck. How much more pathetic was I willing myself to look in his eyes?

He must have sensed my warring emotions because he started asking me questions about myself. My hometown, if I went to college, my friends. I gave him the basics, telling him about friends the most. Beautiful and a little mean, Summer, who had befriended me as a new girl in a small town. Her cousin, Autumn, who was the opposite in every way, blissfully naive and a bleeding heart who would go through the trash at parties to pull out the glass and plastic for recycling. Devin, the artist who was always lost in her own world.

I would have expected him to interrupt me, to have his eyes to glaze over as I talked. But, instead, he leaned forward, watching me. Realizing I had been babbling for far too long, I changed the subject. "I liked Marta. She reminded me of Autumn's mom. Growing up, she was like a second mom to me."

Adrian's eyes softened. "She's great. She and my Gran were friends for a long time. I spent a bit of time at her house with my grandparents."

"Were you raised by them, then?"

He blinked a few times at the question. "No—well, kind of. If you want to get technical, my parents raised me. That was my official address and all, but I spent more time at my grandparents' than at home." He paused, his words careful. "I was a surprise for my parents. They weren't planning on having kids in the first place and were in their forties when I came around."

A pang hurt my chest at what was underneath his words. A long silent moment passed, as if he were considering my question. "But my grandparents were always there. So, physically and financially, yeah, I had parents. But it's my grandparents I was closest to."

"Are they still around?"

He cleared his throat, then took a large drink of his beer. "No, they passed a while ago. Within two months of each other. Gran first and then, without her, my Gramps just faded away." A small smile ticked up on the corner of his lips as his voice grew wistful. "Gramps told me that maybe if I was real lucky, someday I could find someone who loved me half as much as he loved my Gran. But I'd need to get my head out of my ass to find her."

He laughed to himself, and I smiled at the remark. "He sounds like a good man."

"He was. They both were." His eyes focused back on me as if he were realizing who I was. "Wow, sorry. I haven't told anyone about that before."

Reaching out, I placed a hand over his. "I don't mind."

He studied my hand on top of his, and I wondered if he was going to push me off. Instead, he turned my hand until it was facing up. With the lightest touch, he traced a circle around the inside of my palm. Every brush of his fingertip sent heat down my arm and into my chest. My ribs too tight with the expanding sensation, almost to the point of pain.

"I wonder why you're so easy to talk to." His question didn't feel like it was directed at me, more a musing to himself.

He wouldn't look at me, still tracing on my hand. A circle, a star, small shapes. Each glancing touch throws me more and more off balance. The late '90s rock music fell away.

"Easy to be with," I murmured, so low I wasn't sure he could hear me. His fingers moved from my palm to my wrist. The thin skin of the inside of my arm heated at his gaze.

A loud thud of the door opening startled us apart, cold air blasting through the small bar. A group of men came in, loudly joking about the Seahawks chances for the playoffs.

Tucking my hand under my leg, I ignored the phantom of his touch on me. Adrian let out a low chuckle, glancing at the door while he finished his beer.

I followed suit, chugging the rest of the winter ale.

"Another round?" he asked as he stood up from the table.

I nodded, not trusting my voice not to betray me. My smile shaky as he walked back to the bar. What was happening to me? Over the years, I had crushes on men, fleeting things, where I would talk a little too much or laugh a little too hard at their jokes. I thought I knew what it was to be attracted to someone. But I had never in my life had such a visceral reaction to a man. In all the years I spent in relationships, no one had ever affected me the way Adrian did from a simple hand-holding.

There was an intimacy between us that was frightening. I never put stock into my mother's sense of intuition, but everything in me was telling me that being beside Adrian fit. For years, I swallowed down the annoying voice in my head that something wasn't quite right. No relationship could be perfect, so why nitpick things? But it was right with Adrian.

Shaking my head, I tried to get the idea out of my mind. I didn't know this man. I was rational, sometimes. And didn't need to get attached to a stranger.

From my spot at the table, I watched as Jordan, the bartender, leaned across the bar top. I couldn't hear everything that was said, but I was sure I caught the word "man whore." Adrian flipped her off as she turned away to refill our drinks. He could flirt with whomever he wanted. Was I developing a small crush on my vacation house neighbor? Yeah, obviously. But I was a grown woman.

Sometimes.

While he was at the bar, I walked down the bright purple hallway to the single-person bathroom. A chipped mirror hung over a pedestal sink that had a brown ring of soap scum in it. The walls were decorated with people's phone numbers, multiple anarchy signs, and the word "cocksucker" five times over.

I focused on the signs on the lime green walls—*Hey, Diddle Diddle, Aim for the Middle!* and *Best Seat in the House*—anything, but my shaking hands and the lump in my chest.

The soap was thin pink sludge that made my hands feel dry as I was washing them. The knob stuck as I tried to turn it. It took some aggressive jiggling before I either broke the lock or opened it. The door jamb was in bad enough shape with gouges all over that it was hard to tell what I did and what had already been there. Walking back out into the almost empty bar, Adrian was still talking to the bartender. She was pretty. Short, straight black hair, and a lip piercing. Colorful tattoos covering her arm and up her neck.

I got my belly button pierced a year into my relationship with Buck, and he insisted that a classy woman would have only a single ear piercing on each ear, so I let the hole close up. Tattoos were a definite no-no. Maybe I'd get a tattoo. I hadn't allowed myself to think about it, but the idea appealed to me. A few feet away from the table, an arm reached out, stopping me in my path.

"Well, aren't you a pretty thing?" The man set his beer down directly on the bar top instead of a coaster. A faded beanie covered his head and a scraggly goatee on his chin. He wasn't bad-looking, but I got an icky vibe from him.

I stepped back. "Um, hi."

"I'm Jarrod. I've never seen you here before."

"Because I'm visiting." I glanced over at Adrian. He laughed at something the bartender said, and she flapped the towel at him.

"From where?"

My eyes snapped back to the guy. "Somewhere not here."

I hoped my harsher tone would be deterrent enough, but instead, he laughed. "No need to get testy. We don't get a lot of new people in here. Most of the tourists stay in the downtown area."

"So I've heard." Hugging my purse closer to my chest, I backed up a step, but the man's arm was still in the way, his hand resting on an iron railing separating two areas. Gritting my teeth, I tried to make my words as clear as possible. "Please move your arm so I can get back to my friend."

"Which friend?" the man glanced around, his eyes stopping on Adrian and Jordan. "Looks like your friend is busy."

An embarrassing heat flooded my face. Swallowing down the sensation, I straightened my shoulders. "I need to go back to my table."

"Aw, playing hard to get. I like that in a woman."

That was enough. Crossing my arms over my chest, I glared at him. "And you're playing hard to get rid of. Move your arm. Now."

"No need to be like that. I'm trying to get to know you."

"She said move, Jarrod." Adrian appeared on the other side of me.

Jarrod's pale face turned red at the sight. "Well, hey, Winter. We were just chatting. Weren't we, beautiful?"

I didn't respond, instead glaring at him.

Adrian pushed Jarrod's hand off the rail and grabbed my hand, pulling me toward him. His arm laced around my waist as he bent down to press a kiss to the top of my head. "Come on, Birdie."

I knew it was more show for this guy than anything, but damn if I didn't fit right into the crook of his arm. Wrapping my arms around his middle, I leaned into him as he walked me away. He smelled so good. That warm fire and spice scent I would now always associate with him.

Once settled at the table, Adrian moved his seat until his knees were bumping against mine. He was slightly facing Jarrod, a scowl on his face. I took a small sip of the beer in front of me. "Took you long enough."

He grimaced. "At first, I was seeing what you'd do. I wasn't sure if you were interested in Jarrod over there." He tapped a finger on his lips. I watched the motion. His lips were soft. I bet they would feel nice under my fingertips. They sure felt good on my head.

I glanced at the man behind me, his shoulders slumped over his now empty beer glass. "Uh, no. I'm not."

"He's not normally a bad guy."

"Does he really seem like the kind of guy I'd be interested in?" I asked.

"I don't know what kind of guy you're interested in. I don't know you."

Blinking a few times, I let his words soak in. He was right; he didn't know me. Hell, I didn't know myself.

"You didn't have to turn him down on account of me."

His blue-green eyes bore deep as he frowned down at me.

"Didn't I?" The words came out softer than I planned. His eyes flickered down at my lips, and a heavy sensation formed in my gut as I leaned closer. "I spent years with a guy exactly like that. I don't want that guy."

"I don't think you know what you want." His body closer now, the heat of him through that gray henley shirt radiated toward me. My hand twitched at the impulse to rest on his chest.

"I know exactly what I want." I let out a shuddering gasp, realizing that I was getting too close to crossing a line. "But what I want and what I need are two very different things. And despite what my best friend was urging me to do, a one-night stand is not at all what I need."

He tucked a lock of hair behind my ear, his fingers brushing my jaw. As he leaned forward, I thought he might kiss me, but his face bypassed mine. His lips skimmed over my ear, his words quiet and hot on my skin. "Aren't you a good girl?"

My knees were weak, and I fought the urge to grab his arms for stability. He leaned back. I grabbed my beer, taking a large swallow. If I focused on the beer and didn't look at him, maybe I could stop myself from jumping him in the middle of this dive bar.

We took identical sips of our beers, our movements mirroring each other. A smirk ticked up on the corner of Adrian's mouth as he lowered his glass to the table. A small piece of foam clung to the left corner of his lip.

"You have a little—" I motioned to his mouth.

His pink tongue darted out, swiping at the foam but missing a bit.

"No, here." I leaned forward, swiping at his lips with the pad of my thumb. His lips were soft velvet, his day-old beard bristly. As I drew my hand back, he caught my wrist.

With his eyes not leaving mine, he brought my thumb into his mouth, licking the speck of foam off my thumb with his tongue. His teeth scraped against my skin, sending heat down my arm and straight to my core. Would this be how he felt if he kissed me? He sucked my thumb harder into his mouth, circling over it. An image of him kissing a whole other part of my body rushed into my mind.

Around us, the bar was filling up, sounds of laughter and stories. The door would open, bringing in gusts of frozen air around everyone's ankles.

All that fell away as he stared at me, his tongue moving over the pad of my thumb and sparks of awareness lighting on my clit.

It was my thumb, not my breasts or between my legs. It shouldn't have been erotic, but the slow languid strokes of his tongue, the way his gaze never left mine, made me want more. Pulling my hand out of his mouth, he pressed a small kiss to my thumb before giving it back to me.

"Did I get it?" he asked.

I couldn't speak, nodding instead at him.

"Come on, let's get you back to the cabin."

Pulling up to the cabin, I placed a hand on the door, hesitating. Would he invite me in? Should I invite him over for dinner? How do you seduce a grown man? The entire ride up the mountain, I realized I wanted Adrian. I knew it before. Physically, he obviously affected me. But after spending those few hours with him, I knew he was right for whatever fling Summer said it should take to get over Buck.

But to actually do it? The last time I seduced a man, it was asking him to teach me how to shotgun a beer in the fraternity basement.

"Do you want to—" His phone cut him off, and he frowned at the screen before answering.

I could hear a woman's voice on the other end but not what was being said. Adrian listened for a few minutes before saying, "Okay, let me finish up what I'm doing and I'll be over. See you in thirty."

He hung up, shoving his door open and climbing out. Was that his girlfriend? He wouldn't flirt with me if he had a girlfriend, would he? Guys cheat, I knew that. And while Adrian seemed like a good man, that didn't mean a thing if he had someone. While I was running through possibilities, Adrian was at my door, his hand out to help me down.

Having climbed out of the truck twice now, I was fairly sure I could have managed on my own, but still, I took his hand. My feet on the ground, I raised my head to look up at him. Did he have to be so tall?

And sexy, don't forget sexy.

He was still holding my hand, and despite myself, I didn't pull away. Might be the only skin-to-skin contact I was going to get this week. His eyes impossibly deep and sweet as he looked down at me. Heat from his hands radiated up my arm. My legs shaky as he stood so close to me. "Everything okay?" I asked.

This made him drop my hand. Running a hand over his head, he pulled his beanie off, ruffling his hair. "Yeah, I got to run back into town in a few to take care of something."

He stomped away, as if annoyed. The tailgate made a loud noise as it slammed down. He grabbed the four bags of groceries, carrying them all in his arms. A glance at the back of his truck showed me he got all my stuff. I followed behind him to the cabin where he was hesitating on the porch.

Once the door was unlocked, he walked into the kitchen and unpacked my groceries for me. I stood back, watching. He even hung the bananas on the little banana hook instead of throwing them on the counter.

He folded the paper bags, slid them under the kitchen sink, and turned to me. "You good here?"

He was polite, but the warmth and humor from the bar was gone, replaced by a scowl.

"Yeah, totally." I wrapped my arms around my body.

He glanced at my hands, tight on my upper arms. Frowning, he moved to the living room, rebuilding the fire in the stove in a matter of minutes.

"You should be warm enough the rest of the night. Let me know if you need help." He glanced out the window at his truck. "I, hopefully, won't be too long, but I don't know."

Giving him a fake smile, I tried to fight down the rolling in my stomach. "I'll be good. I'm a big girl. Thank you for today. I had fun."

His face softened. "Me too." He hesitated, stepping closer to me. "Maybe I could stop by later?"

A genuine smile blossomed on my face. "I'd like that."

"Hopefully, I won't be too long." I thought for a second he might hug me or something, but instead, he stepped back, leaving the same way he came. Unabashedly, I watched him out the window as he climbed back into his truck and drove off.

After a girl dinner of soft cheese, eggplant spread, crackers, and salami eaten over the sink, I caught up on some work. Strictly speaking, I wasn't taking time off to be here. Since my work was all remote, as long as I got the reports submitted by the due date, they didn't care if I got them done at three a.m. or three p.m. I replied to a few emails and read celebrity news. A supermodel was expecting a baby with her husband. The lead singer of a rock band was spotted at a concert arguing with an unknown woman. The lead actress in a TV paranormal drama was leaving her show that season. A Grammy nominated singer was spotted with a baby bump. I watched multiple videos of a lobsterman cleaning barnacles off lobsters before giving them a fish snack in their claw and throwing them back into the ocean. Played a few rounds of my fruit merge game. Anything to stop me from checking out the window for Adrian's truck. Hours went by, and the sky grew dark.

"Knock it off," I mumbled to myself. I wasn't going to wait around any longer for that man. I went up the loft, opening up my suitcase, I dug through the various shirts and overabundance of clean underwear for my swimsuit. Unzipped the front pocket to see if I had stashed it in there. Nope.

I remembered I found the top and was searching for the bottoms when I got distracted by the breaking from a cult podcast I was listening to.

Crap. I left my swimsuit on the counter beside the library book I was going to bring. With no swimsuit on hand, I sat on the edge of the bed, my teeth biting into my lower lip. I could go in my underwear, but I only had one backup bra.

The hot tub was on the side of the house, only a few steps from the back door to the hot tub. Once I was in the water, there wasn't any way of telling if I was wearing a suit or going naked. It wasn't like I had never skinny-dipped before, and what was this trip but a reclaiming of myself? If I wanted to sit in a hot tub naked, it was my right.

My courage screwed tight. I wrapped a towel around my body and walked down the stairs to the back door. As I walked out the door, the small porch light turned on, blaring yellow bright and blanching the porch. I glanced across the way at Adrian's house. His kitchen light was on, but no others were. His driveway was dark, with no sign of his truck. Even if he were home, I couldn't see him, so there was no way he could see me. It would only be a few seconds of nakedness before the water covered me. I set my can of wine down on the side of the tub. No point in getting a glass out here. One hand clutched the towel around me, the other hand flipped the cover off the hot tub. Wisps of steam and the chlorinated scent filled the air. A quick test of the water proved that the water was hot enough to keep me comfortable in the freezing temperatures.

Before dropping my towel, I took one last glance across the way at Adrian's house. Still, the house was dark. Before I lost my nerve, I flung the towel onto the small hook beside the tub and climbed down into the hot water. The heat enveloped me as the water came up to my armpits. There. I was under, and nothing could be seen, even if Adrian could see over here.

Leaning back against the seat, I reached behind me to grab the can and took a big swig. Truly, whoever came up with the idea to put half a bottle of wine into an aluminum can was a genius. A year before, a woman in Buck's circle of friends had ranted at me about the tackiness of drinking out of a can.

Can you imagine? It's atrocious, the subtle hints of metal and gasoline.

The wine tasted fine to my palate. The $5.99 sticker made it all the more appealing. Darkness had fallen over the house. If it wasn't for the moon's reflection on the snow, I wouldn't be able to see the trees surrounding the property. With my eyes closed, I could hear the low rushing of the Icicle Creek beyond the tree line. I would have to venture down there and look tomorrow. In the pictures on the website, they showed people sitting in tubes in the sunshine, but obviously, river floating was out of the equation on this trip. Still, like many things in this area, I suspected the pictures couldn't do the area justice.

Grabbing my phone from the side of the tub, I turned on my favorite angry-girl rock playlist, letting the screaming vocals and righteous indignation wash over me. My eyes closed, I sang along to the lyrics about being betrayed and getting revenge. No one would ever say I was even a mediocre singer, but here, in the woods, with no one for miles, it was only the deer and the birds who had to suffer through my off-key wailings.

I took a quick picture of the can against the snow and cedar yard and posted it for my close friends. Taking a loud slurp from the can, I wondered what Adrian was doing at that moment. He seemed bothered by the call he had. I would never assume I was the best at reading people, but I got the sense he wanted to stay, even as he was leaving. Was that woman a girlfriend? She was something if he left the way he did. In my experience, a guy won't leave a woman he likes unless he has someone better. He probably had a girlfriend or something. That would be my luck. I guess I was terrible at picking them. Still, at this moment, with no one around, it couldn't hurt to think about him.

Was he thinking of me?

That moment in the bar ran through my head. Would his lips feel as soft as they looked? His hands were calloused and rough as he helped me into the truck. What would those hands feel like on my body?

Setting the almost empty can down on the lip of the tub, I rubbed a finger over my lips. The beer we drank was smooth and dark. Is that what his kiss would taste like? Closing my eyes, I rested my head back, letting my fingers skim over my lips and then down my throat.

No one could see me. I was alone. I could picture any hands on my body. It didn't have to be Adrian's. My nails scratched across my collarbone, sending sparks down my body. Leaning back, my breast came out of the water, my nipples hardening in the cooler air. My hand was his hands, feeling the fullness of my breasts, rough against the peaks. His mouth would kiss down my neck and then he'd take one brown nipple between his lips, rolling his tongue over them.

Slipping one hand under the water, the slickness of my skin gave way to roaming fingers. His hand would be bigger, harder against my flesh. My legs fell apart as I delved between my legs. I wished I had brought my vibrator, but my fingers would have to do until I got back inside. With one finger inside me, I rubbed my clit with my thumb. Would he be fast and hard?

No, Adrian would take his time. My fingers moved in and out of me, edging me closer. I was never good at getting myself off with my hand, but picturing my hand as Adrian's hand, his cock, I was spiraling out. The area was quiet except for the splash of water as I ground my hand harder against my clit. My eyes closed, I could see that devilish flash in Adrian's eyes as he leaned into me.

Aren't you a good girl?

His thick thighs between my own, the tension in his jaw as he stared down at me. His hands on my waist as he pushed deeper.

Good girl.

It was my fantasy, and though I had never been much for dirty talk, the words he would say spurned me forward.

Look at you taking my cock like a good girl.

His mouth on mine, our bodies slick as he pumps into me.

I'm going to make you scream my name.

My hand was no substitution for him. I knew he'd be bigger, take me harder and slower. Still, I fucked my hand as if he were the one inside me.

Come for me, Birdie.

My orgasm rippled through me, an explosion behind my eyelids. The sound of my cries echoed in the trees. Languid, I laid my head against the headrest. My hand felt numb as I eased it from between my legs.

My wet hair stuck to my forehead, a mix of sweat and water. The last time I had envisioned someone was a year before and was a sword-wielding vigilante on a popular streaming show.

My boyfriends through the years had never played a part in my fantasies. In all my years of getting myself off did it happen so quickly and so fiercely. The idea of my temporary neighbor and a few innocuous words, and I was a mess.

With my free hand, I pushed my hair off my face and straightened up. That was fun. Grabbing my can of wine, I brought it to my mouth. As I tipped the can up, my eyes caught on the house opposite me. A silhouette of a man stood in an upstairs window. Without seeing his face, I could feel Adrian's eyes on me.

Adrian

I WAS SO CLOSE to asking Wren to come inside with me when I got the phone call. The entire drive up, I played out all the scenarios in my head. I could offer to make dinner or a London Fog. She ordered one of those at the coffee stand on our way into town. I could look up the recipe for whatever that was.

The hooded gaze she gave in the bar let me know she was as affected by my presence as I was by her. Desperately, I wanted the night to continue. And then I got the call from Penny that Tam had to go to the airport to pick up her parents and that a pipe burst in their basement.

My raging hard-on would have to wait while I helped my friend. Penny was apologetic, offering to send me home with a batch of her cookies, but I refused. Penny was a great woman, but the last time she made cookies, she accidentally used garlic butter instead of regular. I was still recovering from the taste of savory snickerdoodles.

As I pulled my truck onto the street, I cut the lights, not wanting to shine my high beams right into Wren's window. This road was my own, and I could drive it with my eyes closed. I climbed out of my truck, glancing back at the cabin across from me. Loud music was playing somewhere in the house. The light for the loft bedroom was on, and the side porch light was on. As much as I wanted to go straight over there, gunky water sloshed in my boots, and my jeans were soaked through. I couldn't let her see me like this. Maizie jumped up at me, her paws scratching against my thigh as I walked to the back. Shrugging off my coat, I hung it on the coat rack before toeing off my shoes and lining them up under the rack.

Trudging to my bathroom, I peeled my soggy clothes off, tossing them into my washing machine. If I was going to go over to Wren's, I would need to take a quick shower first.

After I scrubbed off the grime and the smell of sulfur, I turned the shower off. Clad in a towel, I walked up the stairs and into my bedroom. Maizie followed behind me, trying to lick at the water on my legs. Not bothering with the lamp on the other side of the room, I grabbed my clothes, pulling them on as fast as I could. I needed to move the switch to beside the entrance. I stepped closer to the window to make sure there were still lights on.

The shirt in my hand dropped to the floor. Tucked in the back corner of the side porch, Wren sat naked in the hot tub. From almost any other angle, I wouldn't have been able to see her, but from above, the single bulb was a spotlight in the most erotic scene I had ever experienced. Wren's hands roamed over her body, pinching her nipple and delving between her legs. Her head thrown back and water sluiced over her skin as she rocked over her fingers.

Clumsy and raw, it was nothing like in porn. It was the single most entrancing thing I had ever seen. I knew it was wrong to watch her, but I couldn't look away. Her mouth opened and closed with words I couldn't make out, and her pace increased. Water splashed over the side of the tub. Her face screwed up tight, and her whole body tensed before she cried out. Eyes still closed, her head rested back against the headrest, a small smile on her face as her body relaxed.

All I could hear was my shaky breath as I tried to get myself to step back and turn away before I was caught peeping on her like some '80s movie villain. But my feet wouldn't move. Still in the tub, Wren sat up, taking a long drink from her can. As she set the can down, her face tilted up, her gaze directly on my bedroom window. Her arm stilled as our eyes caught. It was too far away to tell if she was blushing, but her breasts disappeared under the water until she was submerged up to her shoulders. Her arms wrapped around each other.

Shit, I was a total peeping tom. A voyeur into what was a very private moment. As I was about to turn away, Wren seemed to get a burst of courage. She stood in the tub until the water line was below her pubic bone. In the light, water gleamed over her bare skin. Her breasts were soft and teardrop-shaped. Her hips were full, perfect for holding onto.

Her eyes on my window, she slowly climbed out of the tub, not rushing as she wrapped a towel around her body. With one backward glance at me, she picked up her empty can and phone before disappearing into the cabin.

I don't know how long I stood there, half disgusted with myself and fully turned on. The lights went out in the cabin as I waited for reason to come back to me. I wasn't that kind of man. Wren would probably never want to see me again after I spied on her in that moment. And she would have every right.

Climbing into bed, I pulled the sheet over me and rolled over. It was wrong; disgusting, and devious to be playing the scene over in my head. But still, I reached into my pants, pulling my cock free. I was going to hell for this, but I didn't care. Again and again, I recalled her face, the way the water clung to her bare breasts, the movement of her hands between her legs. Pumping harder and harder, my movement kept time with the image of Wren. It was horrible—I was horrible. But still, I stroked myself until spent on my sheets.

The haze lifted from my eyes, and I looked at the mess I made. Grumbling, I stripped the bed and walked downstairs to start a load. I may be a voyeur for Wren, but sleeping on top of my own jizz was a whole other level of gross.

A wetness on my forehead woke me. Maizie's scruffy face was an inch from my own as I opened one eye. Rolling back over, I took my blankets with me. My eyes shut, I tried to drift back to sleep, but now she was using her little sharp nails on my back.

"Okay, okay, I'm up," I grumbled, rising and pulling on a pair of sweatpants off the floor. Once in the kitchen, I turned on the coffee maker and leaned my butt against the counter. I scrubbed my face, trying to wake myself up, my beard scratchy under my hand. The dog danced around my feet, her tongue dangling out.

"I'll take you out in two minutes. Let me get a cup of coffee first." There were too many eagles, coyotes, and cougars in the area for me to let her roam the woods on her own. Not that she was going to go far in the snow. Her dainty little paws didn't like the cold.

Pulling on my jacket over my bare shoulders, I zipped it up to my chin, and we walked out the side door. Maizie took off down the three steps into the side yard area facing the river. Standing on the porch, I kept the wiry fur ball in my sight as I sipped my coffee. The cool air nipped my exposed skin as the drink warmed me. Sparing a single glance over at the cabin beside me, I saw no movement. Her car was still parked in the same spot, and the lights appeared to be off. The cover was back on the hot tub that was the scene of the night before.

The river was a low roar as I flowed a few hundred feet from my porch. A bird song and the sound of Maizie breaking branches as she walked. My phone buzzed in my pocket, and I opened the text to see that Tam was inviting me out to dinner downtown.

I sent off a thumbs-up and set the phone back down on the railing.

Maizie pranced back, having done her business near a tree. She climbed up on the porch and gave a large shake to dislodge the bits of snow on her fur.

"All that trouble for two minutes?" I asked her as she scratched at the side door to be let back into the warm house. I pushed the door open, allowing her inside. As I was stepping behind the dog, I heard a loud shriek coming from the river.

Setting my coffee mug down on the railing, I ran down the side stairs and toward the river. The weather had warmed enough days before to send torrents down from the top of the mountain. At the foot of the embankment, Wren was scrambling out of the rushing water. Clods of dirt and snow fell over her hands as she tried to pull herself out to safety. Despite walking this path constantly in my lifetime, my feet slid out beneath me. My heartbeat was loud in my ears, and a coldness seeped into my chest at seeing Wren in the water.

Judging the distance, I jumped down into the water, wading toward her. My feet were impossibly clumsy as I struggled to get to her faster.

"Adrian!" Surprise and relief laced her expression as I worked my way to her side.

"Grab me. I'll pull you up." Holding on tight, I grasped her elbows, pulling her up to me until she could stand. The water was still rushing by our ankles, but at least now we were out of the worst of the danger.

Clumps of mud and leaves cling to her sopping wet coat and pants. Helping her move on to the bank, I pointed to a spot a few feet down.

"You'll need to climb up that, but I'll be there behind you in case you slip, okay?"

She nodded, her teeth chattering together as she trudged to the path. One step behind her, I pointed to the spots where the roots made steps for her feet. Her feet slid out once, But I caught her by the hips, steadying her before she took us back down into the river again. Once we got to the top, her teeth were audibly clicking together. Wrapping my arm around her shoulder, I pulled her close to me, towing her toward my cabin.

"W-W-Where are we going?" she gasped out between clacking teeth.

"My cabin. It's closer."

Opening the door with one hand, I pushed her inside to the warmth. Once the door closed behind us, I turned to her. Pulling off her coat, hat, and gloves as fast as I could, I dropped them in a heap on the floor.

"Hold on to my shoulders." Her icy fingers found me, balancing. Kneeling down, I grabbed one of her boots and pulled it off, followed by the second one. Still kneeling down in front of her, I grabbed her soaked jeans, unbuttoned them, and started pulling them down.

"W-W-W-What are you doing?" she shrieked.

"Getting these wet clothes off you. You're going to get hypothermia if you keep them on."

"I c-c-c-can do it," she stammered out, her hands moving to her pants, slipping against the stiff fabric.

"Let me do it," I demanded. I looped my fingers into the waistband of her pants and peeled them down her legs. Throwing them into the pile, I stood up, grabbing the hem of her shirt. "This too."

With the wet shirt now in the pile, I grabbed the closest blanket I had and wrapped it around her shoulders. Leading her to the couch, I sat her down in front of the fire, wrapping another blanket around her lower legs.

As quick as I could, I ran to the dryer, pulled out a change of clothes for me, and threw them on. Next stop was the kitchen to get a hot drink for her. I didn't have time to make something, so coffee, it would be.

Sitting back on my haunches, I handed her the mug, which she graciously accepted, wrapping both hands around the hot surface. She took a small sip and grimaced. "No sugar or cream?"

Scowling, I took the mug from her, fixed the drink, then handed it back to her. She took a bigger sip this time and smiled. A warm, bright thing that gave me an uncomfortable expanding sensation in my chest. A lump formed in my throat as I imagined what would have happened if I hadn't been out there when I was.

My hands on each side of her arms, I rubbed them fast, creating heat to warm her faster.

"You know, there are faster ways you could get me naked."

I stopped, frowning at her. "I don't like blue women. People might give me a hard time about my standards, but being warm is one of them."

Color returning to her cheeks, and the blue fading from her lips, she took another sip of the coffee.

"Better?" I asked.

She nodded. "Yes, thank you."

"Good." I let out a slow stream of air, my tone changing. "Now, do you want to tell me what the hell you were thinking, going so close to a raging river in the middle of winter by yourself?"

She flinched back at my words. "I wanted to see it and—"

"What if I hadn't been there? It's thirty-four degrees outside, Birdie. You could have been seriously hurt. You could have died. Do you have any idea how quickly water can lower your body temperature?"

"It was an accident!" she shouted back at me, wrapping the blanket tighter around her body. "I wanted to see the river. I stepped on something, and the ground fell out beneath me."

Scrubbing a hand over my face, I shook my head. "The river erodes the embankment. You always have to be careful around water, especially this time of year. That's all snowmelt."

"You think I don't feel dumb enough? If you'd like to make me feel worse about my stupidity, get behind me in line."

All the fight left me at her words. She was right. It was an accident, a freak thing that could happen to anyone. She wasn't even the first person I had to help out of that river before. So, why was my reaction different with her?

"I'm sorry. I shouldn't have yelled. But I was just so…"

Scared? There weren't words enough for the panic coursing through me. In my classroom, I've dealt with countless emergencies. Allergic reactions, asthma attacks, kids stapling their thumb on accident, kids stapling their friend's thumb on purpose. I was always calm, collected, and ready to help. Today, I was a mess, fumbling and terrified.

"It freaked me out, too." She slid her hand out from under the blanket to grasp mine. I looked at her small fingers above mine. They were still frosty but better than before. Her voice was hesitant as her thumb traced the back of my hand, scorching lines that traveled into my chest. I moved my hand to hold hers better, palm to palm. "Thank you for helping me. I'm sure I would have been able to drag myself out of the river eventually, but having you there certainly helped."

"I was happy to." I cringed at my words. "Not that I was happy you fell in, just that I was there and I could help you, not that you couldn't help yourself. I know you could have, but I was…"

There I go again, a fumbling mess around her. Where happened to the confident man I'd been the night before at the bar?

A small smile ticked up on her lips at my fumbled words. "I know." She glanced down at our hands for a moment, something sad crossing her face. She pulled her hand back, tucking it under the blankets once more before standing with the blanket still wrapped around her body. Walking over to the pile of sopping wet clothes, she picked up her pants and shirt. "I should head back."

"You're not going anywhere like that. Those clothes are way too wet to put back on. You'll get yourself sick."

If she asked to borrow my clothes, I would have let her, but I wanted her to stay, wanted her near.

She frowned at me. "I need to shower or something, get this river muck off me."

"You can shower here," I offered.

She shook her head. "No, it wouldn't be right. I doubt your girlfriend would appreciate it."

I blinked at her, trying to process her statement. "My what?"

The clothes she had clutched to her chest were soaking through the blanket. "Your girlfriend. The woman who called you and you scurried away for? The one you went to see last night?"

"Penny?" The scoff I let out was ruder than I intended. "Penny is the farthest from a girlfriend..."

"Fuck buddy, friends with benefits, lover. Whatever you want to call her."

"She isn't any of those things. She's a friend. My closest friend's wife, actually. A pipe burst in their basement, and Tam was in Seattle picking up his mom from the airport. I went over to help her."

"So, your friend's wife called, and you just went over there?" She repeated the story back, her tone disbelieving.

"I mean, I consider Penny my friend, too. I met her through Tam, and obviously, Tam and I are closer, because he's more like a brother, but Penny is my friend, too."

"You drop what you're doing to help a friend?" she asked, shifting under her blanket.

I nodded. "Don't you?"

She nodded. "Yeah, of course. But I haven't seen a guy do that kind of stuff for a friend, especially not a female friend."

"Sounds like you need different guy friends." I took the empty coffee mug from the side table, bringing it to the sink before returning to stand in front of the fire. I might not have spent as much time in the water as Wren. But the river's icy grasp wasn't letting me go as quickly as I would've liked. "Well, what would your ex do?"

"Buck?" Her nose scrunched up in distaste. "I don't think I've ever seen a friend call him for help before. Isn't that weird? If I had to guess, he'd tell them to call a plumber or something? Buck wouldn't know what to do with a broken pipe anyway."

One less point for this loser who let her get away.

Her eyes snapped to me. "So, she really isn't a girlfriend or anything like that?"

I shook my head. "There's no girlfriend, friend with benefits, or—what was the last one?—*lover*? I haven't been with a woman in almost a year."

"A year?" she repeated. "You expect me to believe you have this gorgeous cabin in the mountains, you look like that"—she motioned to my body and face—"and you haven't slept with anyone in a year?"

How did we go from her falling into the river to discussing my sex life? Or lack of one. Clearing my throat, I glanced away from her. My eyes caught on a framed photo of my grandparents on their wedding day. "Maybe I wasn't interested in anyone around—"

"No one for a whole year has caught your attention?" She dropped the clothes on the floor and stepped closer to me. The blanket fell off her shoulder. I could see the thin white strap of her bra contrasting against her golden skin. Her curls drying wild around her face.

"I didn't say that."

Lines and snow filled yards and rivers crossed and crossed again. I wasn't going to step back from this. "And I can assure you, when I am interested in someone, I make it known."

She stood, the blanket falling down on the floor. It took all I had not to stare down at her body, my eyes glued to her face. "I'm not cold anymore."

"I see that." I allowed myself a quick glance down her body. Umber skin, smooth and delicate. The small bow of her white bra between her breasts. Her underwear was pink with blue stars—cotton and no nonsense. Having her before me, she was sexier than any lingerie model I had ever seen in a magazine. "You seem warmer."

She cocked her head to the side. "Maybe I will take a shower here."

"Here?"

"Are you going to watch me there, too?"

I grimaced. "I shouldn't have watched you. It was wrong of me. Depraved."

"It truly was." Her voice was husky. Her hand drifted to my arm, the now warm fingers tracing a line from wrist to elbow. "But maybe I'm a little wrong, too. I saw you. You caught me earlier."

Damn how I wanted this woman, but I wasn't going to push her too far. I'd give her the out if she needed it. "You saw half my ass cheek for a few seconds. I watched you...um."

"Yes, you did." She stepped closer, her damp bra brushing against my chest. "Yesterday morning, you knew I was watching you. I could tell."

I nodded at her. "I could feel your eyes on me."

"Last night, I didn't know you were watching me, but..." She hesitated. "If I had known, I'm not sure I would have stopped."

"What are you saying?" My voice now was lower as I raised my hand, brushing a thick curl back over her shoulder. Her skin was softer than all my fantasies could have imagined.

"I would have looked up at your window the whole time and done the same thing." She didn't let that statement settle. Instead, she said the thing that stopped me cold. "But you're not asking the right question."

I stared down at her, the night replaying in my mind. What question? What could she mean? What...Oh. Running a thumb over her lips, I bent lower. "Who were you thinking about?"

Her word was air against my thumb, hot and ready. "You."

CHAPTER SEVEN

Wren

CANNED WINE WAS A mistake. I scanned the empty can in the recycling bin. Not that I was a lightweight. But between the beers at The Horse and Trails, my girl dinner of crackers and cheese, and the hot tub, the can was enough to make me act like a complete idiot.

Did I know Adrian was watching me? Not exactly. But in my buzzed and lusty stupor, I rationalized him watching me as the same as me watching him. I stood up in the tub, flashing him all my goodies. I couldn't see his face. For all I knew, it was his back, and he didn't see a thing. Embarrassment should have overwhelmed me. Instead, as I fell asleep, I pictured he was watching me. That he liked what he saw. And I took care of myself for the second time that night.

I was losing my mind.

With my head pounding, I shuffled out of the bathroom, catching the frightful sight of bags under my eyes. At least I had enough sense the night before to wear my bonnet, so my hair wasn't as bad as the previous morning. My head still pounding, I pulled my bonnet off and fluffed out my hair. Still pounding, why was my head so loud?

Not my head, Summer calling me.

"Hey." Ignoring the daily affirmation that Autumn sent in the group text: *I gift myself with time spent in nature*, I put it on speakerphone. The phone balanced on the counter as I finger combed my curls. "How's London?"

"Wet. So, you're still alive!"

After slathering my face with the vitamin-C serum, I fanned my skin to dry. "Why wouldn't I be?"

"I wasn't sure if you drowned in your can of wine or were carried off by an elk."

"Nope on both accounts."

"How's the hot neighbor?"

I dotted moisturizer on my skin, tapping it into my face. "Still hot and likely has a girlfriend or a fuck buddy or something."

I recounted the events of the day to her, telling her about being caught naked, but not what I was doing. "There's no way he's interested, right? He must be a flirty guy with everyone."

Summer hummed, considering my story. "Yeah, that's a tough one. I mean, what kind of guy sees a naked lady in the hot tub and doesn't want to join her? But maybe he was embarrassed about being caught? Or doesn't think you know he saw?"

"All that doesn't matter if he has a girlfriend."

On the other end, there was a loud conversation and then a sudden quiet. Glancing at the time, I deduced that it was close to dinner time over there.

"Or he could be a good guy who is helping a friend."

Picking up the phone, I walked back up the stairs to the loft to dress. "Right. Weren't you telling me thirty-six hours ago that I only attract terrible guys?"

"No." I heard the soft shuffle of clothes and a zipper. She was likely unpacking. "What I said is that you don't date nice guys. I'm sure you've attracted plenty of nice guys, but you don't end up dating them."

"Well, this guy is way too hot to be a nice guy. It would disrupt the universe of something. He had to have a friends-with-benefits situation at least."

"You could still fuck him, you know," Summer said casually. "If what he has is casual, it's on him to be honorable, not you. Make sure he wraps it, of course, but you can still get that dick."

"You're impossible. You know that?"

"Oh, please, don't act like you weren't thinking about it. You're into him. Why do you have to make it a big thing? Ride him cowgirl style and, in a few days, come home sore and happy. No harm."

"But I've never…"

"Yeah, I know, but this guy sounds like a good bet. I know you. I doubt a man had made you come in years."

Or ever, I corrected.

"And you're leaving soon. A little winter fling before you come back home and figure your shit out."

"I'm not doing anything if he has a girlfriend."

"Obviously."

On the other end, there was a shout and knock.

"Hold on." There was a muffled noise where she was talking to someone. I heard the word pub and a laugh. "Sorry, that was my flat mate. I'll call you back later, Wren. Ta."

We disconnected, and I set my phone down. From the small window in the loft, I could see the river in the distance, the snow-covered ground, stark in the midmorning sun. I had planned on checking that out anyway. A few minutes by the river might help. While I rarely tried out Autumn's affirmations, maybe standing beside the river and being one with nature would calm my racing self-doubt. A minute or two of meditation or quiet thoughts or whatever it was that grounded non-anxious people did. I pulled on my boots.

Wrong path again. If I had stood on the other side of that tree, the ground wouldn't have crumbled beneath me, and I wouldn't have ended up waist-deep in near freezing waters. How Adrian heard me and got to my side so quickly, I wasn't sure but was grateful nevertheless.

Now, standing in his living room, there was a chance this conversation was going in the wrong direction. He might not be attracted to me. There might be a girlfriend he's lying about. There could be a million little reasons I was making a complete fool of myself.

But I was tired of putting myself second. Of wishing for more and settling for the bare minimum.

I let the blanket drop at my feet, stepping closer to him. Watched as his eyes flickered over my body, the hunger in his gaze. Letting go of the fear of rejection, I said those bold words. It took channeling all those sexy women in movies. Women who knew their worth. I could be that woman for a day.

"You."

No sooner had the words left my lips than his mouth descended over mine. His kiss was hard and unforgiving, as his hand tangled in my hair. Despite being in the icy river less than thirty minutes before, my body was all fire. My arms wrapped around his back, pulling his body flush with mine. He was all hard lines against my soft stomach.

Waves of heat licked at my skin as his fingers moved from my hair down my throat. His thumb hooking into the strap of my bra as he moved down my body.

"I want you." His words were hot on my ear. "I've wanted you from that first moment you stood on my porch."

My core pulsed at his declaration. "I want you."

His hands cupped my ass, squeezing it as his kiss deepened. Holding tighter around his neck as his grip tightened on my upper thighs. He wrapped my legs around his waist, and the center of me was flush with him. The thin fabric of my underwear and his sweatpants couldn't hide the sizable length of him. Wrapping my legs tighter, I ground myself into him. With me around his body, he walked across the room.

I had never been with someone who picked me up like this before. A sensation of being completely overtaken filled me. Surrendering myself over to him, I kissed him harder. I needed more, harder.

His lips never leaving mine, he kneeled down on the rug. The soft fibers were at my back as he laid me down in front of the fire.

I was right about my fantasy the night before. He was taking his time, his touch tracing fiery lines over my body as he moved over me.

"Take off your shirt. I want to feel you." I pulled at his hem.

"Aren't you bossy?" He smirked at me.

"You don't like it?" I asked.

"Birdie, you can boss me around like this any day. I'll do whatever you want as long as I can touch you."

In a single motion, he pulled his shirt over his head, tossing it to the side. His mouth was back on my throat, my collarbone, the top of my breasts. Sliding his hand behind my back, I felt my bra loosen. I didn't even know that was something a man could do outside television.

"You're good with your fingers," I said, my legs falling open for him to lie between them.

From his spot at my bare breast, he looked up at me. A storm over his blue-green eyes. "You have no idea yet. But you will soon."

Can a person orgasm from words alone? Words and his tongue on my nipple, teasing and nipping.

My legs wrapped around his waist, and he thrust against me. Even through the fabric, I could feel how we'd fit together. His mouth moved to my other breast, taking my nipple between his teeth and sucking hard.

A loud cry escaped me at the sensations, and the grip on his waist tightened. My hands reached behind him, running down his back to his ass.

"I need more." I gritted through my teeth.

"I don't have a condom," he said against my stomach as he gazed up at me. "Do you have one?"

I shook my head, my voice shaky. "No. I didn't think I'd... you know, meet you."

Doubt flooded through me. It must have been written all over my face. "I'm not asking you to go without." He clarified.

"You're not? But..."

His mouth stopped me, his kisses hard as his fingers skimmed the edge of my underwear. "Don't worry, I don't need to fuck you to make you feel good."

"But what about you?" I asked.

"I'm not worried about me." His finger hooked at my hips and then I was bare to him. "Do you want my mouth or my hand?"

My limited experience with receiving oral was when Buck would spend thirty seconds licking my clit like a cat before announcing himself ready for sex. "I can't come that way."

A wicked smile lit up his face. "Is that a challenge?"

I shook my head. "No, it's a fact. I never have before."

His finger passed over my clit, sparks shooting through me. "That ends today. And in honor of that, I think you deserve both."

My words cut off as he took my mouth, kissing me. His fingers parted my folds, sliding over my entrance and sending a pulse to my throbbing clit.

"You're so wet for me, so ready, aren't you?"

I nodded. I had never done dirty talk before.

One finger slid inside me, and I gasped at the intrusion. His long finger hit a spot I didn't know was there.

I gasped out a curse as he thrust his fingers inside, adding a second one. My hips moved with his motions.

"That's it. Fuck my hand, get yourself there."

His fingers inside me, taking me closer to something I had never experienced. My hands grasped at his shoulders as he moved. His mouth closed over my bare breast, taking one nipple between his teeth lightly, scraping enough to sting before his tongue swirled around the tip. Between his mouth on my breast and his fingers moving inside me, the ache crested into something more. His thumb grazed my clit, a systematic pulse that took me over the edge. I cried out, my nails digging into his back. Flashes of light behind my eyes, my blood pounding in my head, silencing everything except our breathing.

It was as if my entire body were floating, weightless, and buzzing with low energy.

"That was..." I sucked in a shaky gasp, trying a failing for words. What I had in the hot tub the night before, every experience before that. None compared. And this was his hand.

His hand cupped my cheek as he brought my mouth to his in a searing kiss. When he pulled away, his gaze was wide, as if he were discovering something he had never seen before.

"You're beautiful. You know that?"

Heat flamed in my cheeks. "That's what all men say after getting some."

"I don't."

I sat up, grabbed his shirt from the floor, and pulled it over my head. "You don't have to say that. I don't need you to schmooze me to have sex."

"Is that what you think I'm doing here?" He smirked.

Bringing my knees up to my chest, I studied him with a raised brow. "Yeah, obviously, you're superb at being all suave and flirty and sexy, but you don't need to give me false compliments on top of that."

He kneeled in front of me. "Are you making fun of me? Is this some kind of joke?"

I shook my head. "No."

Reaching between us, Adrian took my hands, holding them tight. "I have never felt more out of my depth with a woman than with you. I was a fumbling idiot not thirty minutes ago, staring at you in a bra like a twelve-year-old boy. Nothing about how I'm acting is suave."

"Adrian, be serious." I raised a brow. "We both know what this is between us, and it's fine. There's nothing wrong with a fling, but I'm obviously into you, so you don't have to say what you think I want to hear."

"On my grandparents, I promise you, I'm telling the truth. When I say that you're beautiful, I mean it. I tell you I want you—I mean it. And when I tell you we both need a shower, it's true."

Point taken, we were both covered in river sludge.

My hand in his, he helped me to my feet, leading me into the small bathroom at the end of the hall. The tiling was redone in a white-and-blue motif with little vases painted on the border.

He saw me glancing at the tiles. "My Gran loved Greece. She picked it out."

Reaching inside the shower, he turned the water on, testing the temperature with his hand.

I bunched the hem of his shirt into my fist, wringing it. As he turned to me, he frowned. "Let me know if it's too hot for you."

I tested the water, biting my lip.

"Do you want me to leave?" he asked.

I shook my head. I didn't. It was one thing to be naked in front of him when we were fooling around in the living room, but this was different, more charged somehow.

"I need you to tell me to stay."

With a steadying inhale, I gazed up at him, his eyes that stormy color I had grown to react to. "Come in with me?"

His gaze grew darker as he agreed. I reached between us, running a finger under the waistband of his pants. He didn't move, allowing me to take the lead. Slowly, I pulled his pants and boxers down in a single long move. He kicked them away in the corner. I had seen a glimpse of this body the day before, but having it in front of me was wholly different. Taking my time, I gazed down at the strong panes of his chest and over his flat stomach, stopping at the juncture of his thighs. I felt the hard length of him in the living room, saw the shadow of it the morning before when I caught his backside. He was long and hard, bigger than I had ever seen.

"Oh, wow. Um, does that thing fit?"

He smirked at me. "I'm sure we can find a way."

I let out an incredulous chuckle. "I'm not so sure."

He took a step closer to me, touching the shirt I was wearing. "Can I..." He tugged lightly on the hem. The air inside the bathroom seemed to go up several degrees from his proximity.

"Okay." My voice came out low, throaty.

The shirt slid over my head, and I was bare before him. He motioned to the shower, and I climbed in, with him following behind.

Under the hot spray, I leaned my head back, slicking my hair from my face. On the other side, he watched me as I moved, his hand cupping his hard cock.

The water ran down my body as I stared back at him. How was the water not evaporating off me from this heat? One step forward, and he reached beside me, grabbing a bottle from the shelf.

"Turn around."

A thrill ran right at my clit at the command. My back to him, I heard the little noises of the shampoo and then his hands were in my hair, massaging my scalp. His short nails, scratching, his fingers working through my hair. I let out a small groan. I always loved having my hair shampooed at the stylist but had never had a lover do it for me. His fingers worked over my hair, scrubbing. All the while, his hard cock was rubbing against my ass, reminders of what was coming. Placing a hand on my shoulder, he turned me to face him, tipping my head back to rinse the shampoo. Now his cock was bumping into my hip.

He applied conditioner, working it through my curls. How he had conditioner at his place, I wasn't sure I wanted to ask. He grabbed a clean washcloth, poured body wash over it, and began scrubbing my skin, starting with my shoulder and moving down my body. He made no noise as he washed me, though he seemed to pay special attention to my breasts. From my neck to the tips of my toes, he washed my body, his hands moving over me. Every pass sends flames of pleasure through me. Once he was content with my washing, he tipped my head back again, taking his time on my hair, methodically lifting and separating my strands until they were rinsed.

"My turn," I said, switching spots with him. He was so much taller than me, I motioned for him to kneel on the floor. His face at my belly level, he gazed up at me as I squirted shampoo into my hands, rubbing it into his wet hair. My nails scraped at his scalp, rubbing in the soap. His hands came up behind me, grabbing onto my ass, his thumbs digging into my skin.

As he tipped his head back to rinse, I ran my fingers through his hair. He let out a low, guttural moan that shot straight to my clit. I squeezed my thighs together to trap the sensation.

His hair clean, he opened his eyes to look up at me. Slowly, he leaned forward until his mouth was at my belly button, his tongue coming out and licking the water from my skin. "You taste so good wet."

From their spot on my ass, his hands moved to grip my hips. Still kneeling on the floor of the shower, his mouth kissed over my pubic bone, down the apex of my thighs.

"Lean against the wall," he ordered.

He grabbed one leg and placed it over his shoulder, and his fingers parted me, delving between my folds.

"I told you I can't come that way."

He smirked at me, his finger running over my seam. "What do you want to bet I can make you come all over my tongue in five minutes?"

"What do I get if I win?" I asked, my words shaky as he slipped a finger inside me.

"If I win, you go out to dinner with me tonight—my treat."

"And if I win?"

Another finger plunged into me, hitting that spot he found earlier. My knees buckled beneath me, but his grip was enough to keep me steady. "I try again until I get it right." Then his mouth was on the center of me. Licking and sucking at my clit. With each stroke, he promised me more and meant to use every second on his knees before me.

I slapped the wall, trying to find purchase on the tiles. My legs losing their strength under me. Sparks shot through my body as his tongue swirled over my sensitive flesh. His hands gripped my hips hard enough that it stung. It was as if he were a starving man and I was his feast.

"Your pussy is the best thing I've ever tasted."

Stars formed behind my eyes as his mouth sucked and licked and prodded at me, driving me closer. He hummed against my clit and between the sound of satisfaction in his voice and the vibration. I was losing all control. My hands in his hair, I held his face tighter to me. My cries echoed in the small bathroom as his mouth took me over.

I was going to lose this bet, and I couldn't be happier for it. Light, sound, and sense escaped me as I threw my head back, crying out his name. My entire body was tingling from the orgasm.

As I came down, my body slumped against the wall.

Carefully lowering my leg to the ground, he grinned up at me. "I win."

"This time." I quipped as I opened my eyes to glance down at him. He was studying my body with a frown.

"I hurt you." He pressed a kiss to my hip bone, where his fingers had dug so tightly. He repeated this on the other side. "I didn't mean to."

"I liked it." Grabbing his arm, I pulled him up to stand in front of me. "I wanted it."

"I've never been like that before. You make me lose all control."

Gripping the back of his neck, my lips met his. The kiss was fierce. Matching his words with my own emotions, I wrapped my arms around his waist. His cock standing at attention against my stomach. I had never been this woman before: wanton, confident, and deeply desired. But with Adrian, I held onto the power in his gaze, and I needed more.

"Me too," I whispered against his mouth before I pushed him back against the cold tile and slid to my knees in front of him. Taking his cock in my hand, I stroked down the length of him, the water serving as lubricant.

"You don't have to..." he gritted out as I licked the tip, the water and pre-cum mingling on my tongue. I never enjoyed giving blow jobs before, a warm-up to get the guy hard before we'd have missionary sex on his bed. But everything with Adrian was new and exciting. I wanted his taste on my tongue, to see the tendons in his neck bulge as I swirled around his tip. His low grunts potent, urging me to take him deeper in my mouth.

His hand strayed to my hair, bunching his fist and pulling my head back. "I want to come on your tits."

His hand over mine, he showed me how he wanted me, how he liked to be touched. Wrapping my hand around his length, I followed his lead. One hand still in my hair, he held my face up to his. His thumb strayed from behind my ear to the top of my throat, pressing down as he groaned loudly. Hot streams of cum jet onto my chest, mingling with the water to drip over my breasts. I glanced down, running a finger over a spot and bringing it up to my mouth.

Hauling me up onto my feet, his mouth came crashing against mine. His lips were firm on mine, his tongue sweeping into my mouth. He tasted of me. The slick heat of water and sweat between us. He pulled away. We watched as his hands smeared his cum into my skin. "Beautiful." His thumb grazed over my nipple.

My clit throbbed again. How was it not tired yet? He leaned down, resting his forehead against mine.

The water beat over us as we held each other. "As much as I'd like to stay here in the shower with you, the water heater is old, and we have about two minutes before it's turning icy on us." He motioned for me to step back into the water. "Rinse off, and I'll go next. I don't want you getting cold again."

A tightness clenched in my chest at his offer. I knew it wasn't a big offer, similar to opening the door for me or helping me out of his truck. But it was a foreign notion.

Once out of the shower, I wrapped one of the oversized towels around my body. Through the frosted glass, I could see his outline. His hands scrubbing over his face, and his lean torso arcing back to rinse off. The male form was never something I gave a lot of thought to. While my friends would send each other pictures of shirtless celebrities and giggle at their muscles, I was never all that interested in ogling men. Adrian was my exception. I could have stood there, watching him under the spray of the water for a long time.

He yelped, reaching forward and jerking the faucet handle to the right until the water shut off. The top of the towel gripped tight in my hand. I stepped back, handing him the other towel as he stepped out. He gave me a grin before leaning forward and drying his hair first, with no shame in his nakedness. Why was I shy all of a sudden? He came on my chest only a few minutes before, and now, I was holding onto this towel as if it would protect me.

Damn, what was I going to wear now? The shower was more foreplay than for cleaning, but there was no way I was getting back into my muddy clothes now.

As he wrapped his towel around his waist, he took in my expression. "You okay?"

"Um, do you have any clothes I can borrow?" I asked.

CHAPTER EIGHT

Adrian

THE SHIRT REACHED DOWN to her mid thighs, and she cuffed the sweatpants several times over to prevent them from dragging on the floor. Wren put her arms out and did a twirl. "I'm quite the fashionista right now."

"You can keep them." I sat on the bed, watching her survey herself in the mirror. "You look good in my shirt."

Glancing over her shoulder at me, she smiled that warm, wide smile I craved. "I bet you say that to all the girls."

I opened my mouth, then closed it. How could I tell her she was bringing out a different side of me? Aside from the woman who stole all my silverware years before, no one had ever taken something of mine. And I certainly never offered.

I've never wanted to see a woman wear my shirt or to fall asleep in my bed.

"You want some food?" I asked.

With the flour, salt, and sugar on the counter, I pulled out the rest of the ingredients from the fridge. Holding the old green mixing bowl of my Gran's with its white flowers, I mixed everything together with a wire whisk.

Wren settled onto a stool on the other side of the island. Her hand resting on her chin, she watched me as I heated the butter in the old pan. I poured the mixture into the pan, turning the pan until the batter was spread evenly.

Furrowing her brow, she pursed her lips. "Um. Is that a crepe? You know how to make crepes?"

Watching the batter so it didn't burn, I nodded. "My Gran taught me. She used to make these for me every time I spent the night. When I turned ten, she said I needed to learn how to make them myself."

I laughed at the memory, my Gran standing behind me as I mixed, flour all over the floor and the stove top. The time I dropped the shells into the mixture and she made me pick them out. We still found crunchy bits when we ate those. And all the burned ones. So many crispy, blackened crepes. But she ate each one I made and made my Gramps eat them too, less enthusiastic than she did, of course. "Yeah, we had a few trial-and-error sessions. But now it's the easiest thing for me to make—besides toast."

"She sounds like a wonderful woman," Wren commented. "I wish I could have met her. You must miss her terribly."

"Yeah." My voice broke slightly at her comment. I cleared my throat, swallowing down the lump in it. "She was great. They both were."

The edges of the batter were browning, and I flipped it with my spatula. Hazarding a glance up at her, I blurted. "They would have loved you."

She laughed, tucking a strand of hair behind her ear. "You think so?"

I nodded as I slid the crepe off the pan. The fridge held little for choices of fillings. I should have brought some stuff from the store. "Sweet or savory?"

"Sweet," she responded. Of course she wanted sweet. Quickly, I sliced some bananas, cooking them for a minute until they caramelized. On top of the bananas, I scattered little bits of chopped bacon I had. I filled the crepe, folding it over in thirds.

"Bananas and bacon?" she asked, a brow raised.

"Try it and tell me it doesn't work."

A dusting of powdered sugar on top and a drizzle of syrup, and I slid the plate across the island top. As her lips closed around the first bite, she moaned around the fork. Her eyes grew large. "Oh my. That is amazing."

Inside my chest, it was as if a balloon were expanding at the compliment. "Yeah?"

She nodded this time, taking a larger bite.

I poured the batter into the pan, to make my own crepe. Carefully turning the batter until it was even.

Her hand in front of her mouth, she spoke with a full mouth. "I might need to eat this every day for the rest of my life."

That could be arranged.

Where did that thought come from?

Her finger dipped into a spot of syrup, which she brought up to her mouth to suck it off. Her tongue swirling around the tip the same way it had my cock in the shower.

Now I had a hard-on while cooking brunch. What kind of man was I? She took another bite of the crepe and glanced down at the pan. "Is it supposed to start smoking?"

I moved the pan to the other burner, cursing myself for getting distracted. Ignoring her eyes on me, I dumped the ruined crepe in the garbage and reduced the heat to remake mine.

I hadn't burned a crepe in over a decade.

Plating my much less extravagant crepe, I sat beside her at the island, our knees bumping as we ate. Maizie wandered over from her spot on her bed, positioning herself between our feet and watching up for tiny scraps to fall. Little beggar.

"So, you open doors for ladies, cook a mean crepe, and you own separate shampoo and conditioner. Will the surprises ever cease?" she asked, setting her fork down.

Growing up, my parents were gone so much I had to learn to fend for myself. I couldn't understand what was surprising for her. Imagining what kind of guys were in her life that holding the door open would be a reason for celebration. "I got to say, as much as I enjoy impressing you with my skills, these are basic things. I know how to do them. Why shouldn't I?"

With a furrowed brow, she got quiet.

Instantly, I worried I had said too much. "These are ordinary things. I don't want to scare you away, but I can't be ordinary for you. You are exceptional. You deserve more."

"You're not ordinary to me." Her voice was low. Her eyes grew soft as she reached out and took my hand. "You're the opposite. You are constantly surprising me."

Lacing her fingers with mine, I brought them up to my lips, pressing a kiss on the back of her hand.

Our stomachs full, I pulled her to the couch, tucking her into the inside before lying beside her. I figured, if someone rolled off the couch, it should be me. My hand on the dip of her waist, I closed my eyes.

What I wanted to say hung back in my chest.

I want to be enough to deserve you.

What was this woman doing to me for these impulses to take hold of me? I shook my head as if that would bring back my sense of reason.

Nope. I was doomed.

Beneath my arm, our bodies grew heavier, and as her breathing evened out, I felt myself drift away.

My phone chimed from its spot on the floor. Ignoring the noise, I buried my nose into the crook of Wren's neck. She smelled of soap and sugar. My eyes still closed, I took another deep inhale of her. I had fallen asleep beside women before, but something about this felt right. The warmth of her body pressed against mine, the way her feet rested between mine. The tickle of her curls against my forehead felt like an idealized version of my life. As if I could dream up what the perfect sensation would be and hold it in my arms.

A scraggly head popped up from between Wren's stomach and the back of the couch. Maizie and I watched each other for a minute. I didn't normally allow her on the couch, as she shed terribly.

The phone chimed again, not ready to be ignored. I scrambled on the ground for the phone.

With one eye, I read the text and groaned. "Crap."

Beside me, Wren stirred. Turning her body to face me, she displaced Maizie, who hopped over us both and climbed onto her dog bed with a disdainful glare.

Her eyes sleep-glazed, she wrapped an arm around my middle and let out a low hum. "What's up?"

I ran a hand over my face. "I forgot about dinner."

Her hand stilled from its spot on my lower back. "Dinner?"

He lowered my head to look at her. "With Tam and Penny. I told them I'd meet them tonight for dinner and drinks. They wanted to thank me for the burst pipe debacle."

Her eyes darted away, her hand tensing. "Right, okay." She started pulling herself up to a seated position. "I'll let you get ready to see your friends. I should get back any—"

"Come with me?" My arms tightened around her waist, pulling her back down beside me. "Please, I want you to meet them."

"You want me to meet your best friend and his wife?" Incredulity laced her question.

Brushing a curl away from her face, my fingers laced into her hair at her nape. I hoped she'd say yes. "You'll like them. Tam is great, and Penny doesn't know how to stay out of people's business, but she's also the warmest person ever."

"You know I'm leaving in a few days, right? I don't want this to get too complicated."

She still thought this was a fling?

Despite her ticking all the boxes, out of towner, no ties to this place? This wasn't some dalliance for me. There had been flings, more than I wanted to share, but nothing about how I felt for her seemed fleeting. There was a shift in me while in her presence. I wanted to buy her dinner and have her meet my friends. I wanted to lay her down on my bed and feast on her body until she couldn't scream any longer.

I didn't know what to call this, but I knew it wasn't a fling.

"Let me worry about complicated. I want you to come out and have fun, no strings, no obligations."

The words tasted wrong on my tongue, but I allowed them anyway. Who was I hurting but myself?

Hesitating, she pulled her lower lip between her teeth. I reached over, pulling that lip out, running the pad of my thumb over it.

"I bet you that you'll have more fun tonight than in the last six months."

She smiled at me, pressing a kiss to my thumb. "What do I get if I win?"

"I'll make crepes tomorrow morning and deliver them to the front door of the cabin."

A small smirk ticked up on the corner of her mouth. "And if you win?"

"I'll make your crepes, but they'll be delivered to you in my bed."

Sliding her hand from its spot on my lower back, she placed it between us. "Shake on it."

The bet secured. She glanced down at herself. "If I'm meeting your friends tonight, I need to go back home and change."

"Why? You look good in my shirt."

She laughed, loud and warm. "Nice try. You might think this is cute, but I can assure you it is not. When are we leaving?"

I checked the clock on my phone. We had napped for the better part of three hours. "In an hour and a half?"

She slid out from under my arm. "I better get to work, then. See you back here soon."

With an ear scratch for Maizie and a searing kiss, she left me alone on the couch. When the door shut behind her, I picked up my phone to call Tam.

"I need to add another person to the reservation."

Tam paused, a heavy metal hitting metal sounding. Likely a tool for fixing the pipe. "Who?"

"Someone I want you to meet. Her name is Wren."

Tam was silent on the other end for a moment before the metal clanged again. "Okay, cool. See you there."

That's what I liked about my best friend. He didn't interrogate me.

Wren

W HAT ARE YOU SUPPOSED to wear to dinner with the friends of your one-night stand? Is that even an apt description of what Adrian and I had going on? It was fully in a vacation fling territory, but he wasn't on vacation. This was his hometown, his friends.

Not that I brought a ton of options. Pulling out a blue sweater and then a gray one, I laid them on the four-poster bed, considering my options.

Why would he want me to meet his friends?

The blue one was softer and low cut, but I liked the way the light-gray one had a low back.

What would they think of me?

If I wore my lacy camisole with the gray one, that could be pretty.

Did he often have women meet his friends?

I wouldn't be able to wear a bra, but that was okay.

What did he think this was between us?

I could pair either with jeans, and they'd be nice enough for anything in town.

Were his feelings growing the way mine were?

Sinking beside my suitcase, I glanced at myself in the floor-length mirror. What was I doing? It had been years since I worked myself up over a man. My hair was a riot of untamed curls. A shower at his place seemed like a good idea in my lust-filled haze, but without my products, my hair was rebelling worse than a petulant child.

Hair tamed first, then clothes.

Working the defining crème into my hair, my curls took shape. It wasn't as good as if I had used the right products in the first place but looked ten times better.

From its spot on the wooden nightstand, my phone chimed with a call. How the phone wasn't destroyed in the river, I wasn't sure but thank goodness for inner-zipper pockets in waterproof jackets.

I glanced at the screen, expecting it to be Summer, to see my mother's picture flash.

"Hi, Mom." The phone wedged between my shoulder and my ear. I rooted around in my suitcase for the camisole.

"Wren, I just had the most bizarre conversation."

"Oh?" Finally finding the top I wanted, I held it up, shaking it a few times to get the bigger wrinkles out. It would have to do.

"Beaufort called us, worried sick about you. Apparently, he's been calling you, but you haven't been answering."

"I blocked his number, Mom. There is no reason he needs to call me."

"Well, he's concerned something happened to you."

"I'm not sure why. He's not my boyfriend anymore. He dumped me, remember?"

"It's hard to tell from such a brief conversation, but I get the impression he regrets that decision."

More like he regrets not having someone tidy up his shoes every night.

"Did he need anything?"

My mother sighed, and I could picture her on my Aunt's back porch, a teacup beside her, wearing her linen pants and flowy embroidered shirt. "Not that he mentioned, no. But it's just a sense that I have. You know how I get those."

My mother's "senses" had about a sixty percent accuracy rate. I was pretty sure it was the same intuition everyone had, but she liked to assign some borderline psychic ability to it.

"Mom, you can hear I'm fine. I'm meeting up with some friends..." Adrian's friends, but I didn't want to send her into a tizzy about my being alone in this cabin. "I should start getting ready."

"I still don't understand what happened with you two. I sensed he was the one for you..."

Drop that accuracy down to fifty-five percent now.

"...and a nice big wedding. Even if his father is a Cougars fan. He was such a nice boy. I suppose we could have overlooked that."

"Mom. We broke up. Buck dumped me, and I am fine. Better than fine, actually."

"He sounded so sad and scared when he called."

"Mom." My voice was sharper now. "He dumped me. I am not responsible for that man's emotions any longer. I love you, but I have to go."

She huffed loudly into the receiver, and I had to pull the phone from my ear. "No need to get testy, Wren Alyse."

"I'm not testy. I'm running behind. Give Dad a hug and let Aunt Cathy know I miss her."

From where I was standing, I could see the sliver of light across the walkway between the two houses, Adrian stepping out onto his front porch. Maizie followed him out, lacing around his feet. He was glaring down at his dog, opened the door wider, and pointed inside. The dog sat on one of his boots, her tongue out.

"Are you with Summer? You know that girl is too wild for my tastes, always has been. I know she was raised with all those big cousins, but she is a bit of a heathen."

Dodging the question, I pulled the sweater on over the camisole and then lay on the bed, tugging the jeans over my hips as fast as I could. When I hopped up to zip them, I saw Adrian closing the front door, this time, dog-free and stepping down the stairs.

"I'll call you later. Love you." I hung up before she could say anything else. I loved my mom, but her idea of what was good for me was as misguided as the years of hair straightening treatments she subjected me to as a child. Before I could tell myself I was jumping the gun, I threw a few overnight things in a small bag. In case things went well, I could grab them later.

Even though he knew the code for the front door, I heard three solid knocks against the wood. I tried to walk down the stairs as fast as I could without sounding like a herd of elephants. I always was heavy-footed.

Opening the door, Adrian stood on the other side. I glanced down at his outfit and let out a small laugh. He was wearing jeans and a light-gray sweater in an almost identical shade to mine.

"We match." A smile lit up his face.

"We do." I opened the door further, beckoning him in. "I just need to swipe some mascara on and then we can leave."

He followed me into the space, his hands wrapped around a black jacket.

Seeing my eyes on it, he held the coat out. "I figured the chance of you bringing a backup jacket was slim, and yours is probably still air-drying, so I grabbed this out of my closet on the way out."

Taking the coat from him, I stared down at the jacket, fighting the lump forming in my throat at the gesture.

"You don't like it? It was my Gran's, and I know the style isn't very fashionable right now, but I didn't want you getting cold and thought—"

I cut off his words with a kiss, pouring all my mixed-up emotions into the embrace. The coat was unfashionable, black, and bulky, with a garish orange-and-blue plaid lining. But knowing before he left his house, he thought of me, I hadn't realized how starved I was for that level of care. When was the last time someone took care of me in this way?

Three days—two and a half days, really. That's all I have.

Pulling away, I hoped my eyes weren't shiny with tears. That would be too embarrassing. "It's wonderful. Thank you."

Needing some distance before I humiliated myself further, I retreated to the bathroom. My makeup bag out, I dug around for the basics. "Sorry, I don't have time for more of a full face," I commented as I applied some cream blush to my cheeks. "My mom called, and I got distracted."

"Wear makeup, don't wear makeup. You are beautiful, no matter what."

Leaning against the doorframe, he took up so much space. Even in the terrible bulb lights of the small bathroom, he was sexy.

Don't get distracted. Don't get attached.

I turned back to my reflection, swiping the mascara on.

I saved the red lip for last to match my nails. Adrian seemed to like it when I reapplied at the restaurant earlier. Or I had lipstick on my teeth, and he was too kind to tell me. Either way, he was staring at my mouth a lot.

"Ah," he murmured, and I glanced over at him.

"What? Do you not like it..."

"The opposite. You are utterly kissable. It's just that I know I shouldn't kiss you and mess up that masterpiece."

I fanned my lips to dry, staring at him. "This is supposed to be smudge-proof when it dries, so maybe we'll have to test it..."

"Really?"

"Kiss proof, food proof, blow job proof." Tapping my lips, I check to find no lipstick transfer. I held up my finger to show him.

"Don't say stuff like that, or I will have to cancel on my friends and take you right here on this bathroom floor."

Smirking, I pushed past him, shrugging on the oversized winter coat. "Let's save that for later."

Dinner was an intimate setting at the local steakhouse. The food was good and the conversation warm. All my concerns about meeting Adrian's friends melted away mere minutes into the dinner. Tam and Penny were easy to talk to. It was as if I had known them for years. They were careful not to tell stories about the past without explaining the context and asked me millions of questions about myself. With Tam's job running a local sporting goods store and Penny as the bookkeeper for the business, I felt comfortable telling them about my work in data analysis. They teased Adrian about his excessive polo collection and how much he talked about Maizie.

Throughout dinner, Adrian kept touching me. A hand on my knee, a bumping on his shoulder. I told an embarrassing story of when I was trespassing at my old elementary school, fell off a fence as I was climbing, and sliced myself behind my ear, needing seven stitches. When I mentioned that the scar tissue made the area numb, Adrian leaned over and pressed a small kiss to the scar.

"Can you feel that?" he whispered in my ear. Heat flooded through me, and I had to cross my legs. Across the table, Tam and Penny smirked at each other.

When I tried to pay for my portion, I was the one who fixed the broken pipe after all. Tam and Penny waved my card away, insisting I could get the next one.

Not likely.

After dinner, they insisted we needed to go to the local bar for a nightcap. Once there, I bought the first round, something they begrudgingly accepted. Snug beside me at a table in the back, Adrian's arm was wrapped around my shoulder. I fit perfectly tucked beside him.

One drink turned to two and then Adrian and Tam left us at the table to get the next round. The moment the guys were out of earshot, Penny scooted from her spot and plopped down beside me.

"Okay, I want to hear all about you and Adrian. Tam had no information, and I was so pissed at him for not getting the details."

"The details?" My voice wavered.

"Yeah, he comes into the kitchen and tells me to add another person to the reservation, so I'm asking him, 'Who is it,' 'Do we know you,' 'Where are you from,' 'Where did he meet you, 'Are you dating,' and he had *no answers*! He didn't ask any of those questions. I love my husband, but he is the worst at information. As though he doesn't even care about his friend's wellbeing. If I had known that you were who he was with last night, I never would have called him about the pipe, but it ended up good for all of us, don't you think?"

I wasn't sure if Penny took a breath during the entire line of questioning.

"Where do you want me to start?" I asked, laughing.

"What white witch magic did you inflict on my friend?" Her smile was warm as she leaned closer.

I laughed at the question. She was still leaning close, waiting for an answer. "Oh. None."

"No affirmations or crystals. Singing Stevie Nicks or Florence Welch while you were driving up here?"

"'Shake It Out' is my favorite song, but that's immaterial. As much as my friend Autumn would love for me to do affirmations, I can't take them seriously. The last thing I expected on this trip was to meet some like…well, Adrian."

Penny narrowed her eyes at me. "Hmm. I'm not so sure you didn't do a little naked dancing in the moonlight. Because that man"—she pointed at Adrian's back as he was talking to a few people at the bar—"has never brought a woman around for a double date."

I fought back the promise of more the statement gave me. "I'm sure you've met other women he's been with before."

"Not a one." She put her finger up in a pause gesture. "Nope, I take that back. I bumped into some snow bunny a few years ago sneaking out of his apartment when he lived downtown. But that doesn't count, as I'm pretty sure neither Adrian nor I caught her name."

A low rolling tension formed in my stomach. I took a small sip of the dregs of my beer. I couldn't put any more hope in what Adrian and I had. This wasn't forever. It was for a week.

"So, tell me, Wren Alexander of Ridgewood, what are your intentions with him?" Penny set her wineglass down, her eyes on Adrian and Tam at the bar.

Busying myself with finishing my drink, I tried to come up with words. I wasn't going to spill my desires with his friends. Penny was nice enough, but if I told her the burgeoning affection I had for Adrian, I would end up being a cocktail party story of that woman who got too attached. I'd be on the same level as the woman who left the dog but took the silverware. I couldn't control exactly how I appeared in someone else's story, but I could try to leave with some dignity intact. "He's a nice guy. We're having fun."

"Fun?" she echoed.

"Yeah, fun. I got out of a super-long relationship a few months ago. I'm not trying to get him to be serious about me or anything."

Penny narrowed her eyes at me. "Anyone between Adrian and this long-term loser? A date or two? Bass player, line cook, podcast host?"

Grimacing, I set my drink down. "There was this one guy I went on a few dates with back home. He actually asked me out in the parking lot of the grocery store. He had great hair, but aside from that, he wasn't anything to include in a dating synopsis."

Penny slapped her leg triumphantly. "Ha! The dusty ex-boyfriend effect."

My confusion must have been all over my face because she kept talking. "You know! You have the long-term boyfriend you think you'll marry, and that doesn't work out, so you go out with some sleazeball a few times and then BAM! You meet your husband."

"Husband?" I choked on my drink, coughing. "I barely know Adrian. We've only spent forty-eight together, max."

"Doesn't matter. It's irrefutable, a canon event. Can I be a bridesmaid?"

Glaring at her, I considered how well she and Summer would get along. They both loved giving me a hard time. Tam returned, holding three drinks in his hands, setting them on the table between us. "Who's a bridesmaid."

"Oh, now you want information," Penny said with a raised brow. "Last night, you didn't need to know a thing, but tonight, you're a detective."

Tam ignored Penny with a well-meaning frown. "Adrian got caught by a former student. He'll be right back."

I glanced over at the bar, expecting to see Adrian talking with a young man, and sharply inhaled. This girl was gorgeous. Long white blonde hair, perfectly straight and down to her elbows, one of those small cupid bow mouths. And even from across the bar, I could see how light-blue her eyes were. Those light-blue eyes sparkled as she leaned into Adrian, laughing at something he said. Her hand rested on his forearm and wasn't budging.

"A student?" I asked, trying and failing to keep my tone balanced. A clammy tingle started at my fingertips watching Adrian and this young lady.

I told myself that he was charming, a flirt, and that didn't translate to infidelity. But seeing Adrian, the way this woman leaned into him, the light touches on his forearm. It was all too much. My breaths came out shallow and shaky. I had no claim on Adrian. Why should I care so much about this barely legal girl trying to pick him up?

Adrian's jaw was tense as he glanced away from the woman. As his eyes caught on me, something dark flashed in his eyes. Guilt? Why should he feel guilty?

I shouldn't be watching him, assigning every gaze and the tilt of his body a meaning.

Adrian gave the woman a small smile and stepped away. The woman's eyes watched him as he walked toward me, her gaze moving from his back to me sitting in the corner.

He set my beer down before me as he slid in beside me. "Sorry about that. I got caught up."

My hand was shaky as I picked up the beer and took a long sip. I wasn't going to be jealous. I had no claim. I wasn't...

"Hey, you okay."

Swallowing the beer, I set it carefully on the peeling cardboard coaster. My eyes stayed on the foam ring around the lip of the glass. Little white bubbles pop, pop, popping as the beer settles.

"Yeah, totally." I gave him what I hoped was a casual smile. Inside, my ribs felt too tight for my lungs.

They began talking, but from the corner of my eye, I could sense the girl watching us, waiting for her chance with Adrian. When he placed a hand on my knee, my stomach rolled with the implication. He flirts with another girl in front of me and comes back here and places and touches me so intimately? I went through years and years of this. While I wasn't going to pretend that Adrian and I had a future, at the very least, I could have some dignity tonight.

"I need some air." The chair made a screeching noise as I scooted back. I stalked past the growing throngs of people filling the bar. Once outside, the crisp air stung my heated face as I leaned against the side of the building.

One deep exhale, two. My finger on my scar, I rubbed the little spot, soothing myself until my breathing steadied. Who was I kidding? I had no idea how to do a casual fling. I spent thirty hours with this man, and I was already getting upset about some twenty-two-year-old making eyes at him? This wasn't me. It couldn't be.

Closing my eyes, I leaned my head back against the bricks. From where I stood in the alley, the sound of the bar was filtering through the occasional opening of the door.

"Wren?" Adrian's voice broke the dull roar in my head.

Startled, I jumped away from the wall, my hand on my chest. "Hey. I'm here."

He rounded the corner, his eyes narrowed as he took me in. "What are you doing out here?"

"I needed fresh air."

"Is that all?"

I feigned nonchalance. "Yeah. Do you need me to call a cab or something to take me back?"

Furrowed brow, he leaned back from me. "A cab? Why would you need a cab?"

I could be cool. I had no claim on this man, and if he wanted to go home with that gorgeous girl with her long blonde hair and small ankles and non-scarred ears, then he had every right.

I motioned to the bar. "If you want to spend more time with your"—I waved my hand in the air, failing for words—"friend."

Adrian snorted. "Layla? She's a kid. I was her teacher."

"She doesn't look like a kid to me."

"Well, she is to me."

"She doesn't seem much younger than me."

"Even if you were the same age—which you're not—I could never get involved with a former student."

I wasn't sure why I was giving him an out. Justifying him hooking up with a student, but the words wouldn't stop. Maybe I needed him to be flawed, to be as uncaring as all the previous men I had known. That way, when I had to leave, I could know I wasn't missing out on something special. "Why not? It's not illegal. She's in a bar. She's obviously of age."

"Just because something is legal doesn't make it okay. I could never cross that line with a student, former or current. To me, they are all the same."

Stepping out from the wall, I faced him, my eyes raised to meet his. "She seems pretty into you."

"I don't care how she feels. Do you think I'd be interested in a girl like that when you're around?"

Shaking my head, as if that would knock some sense into me, I fought for the words.

"If you think I have any interest in another woman when you are next to me, you are blind." Taking my silence for what it was, he grabbed my hand, pressing it against the bulge in his pants. "Feel that. You do that to me. No one else."

I tensed my hand against the form, pressing into it. "Only me?"

He hissed at the contact. "Only you. From the first moment I saw you on my porch, you are all I can think about. You are driving me wild. I've never needed a woman and then you show up, and I can't think, can't talk. All I want is to strip you bare and sink into you."

Wrapping a hand around the nape of my neck, he brought my mouth to his. The kiss was a brutal thing. A punitive nip at my bottom lip as he whirled me around and then my back was to the bricks. My jeans were unzipped, and his hand was cupping my pussy.

"Fuck, you're so wet for me." His finger swept over my entrance. Zinging up my body as he thrust into me. "I bet I could take you right here, couldn't I?"

My hands found his shoulders as he moved against me, the heel of his hand pressing against my clit as he added another finger inside me. My nails dug into the fabric of his shirt.

"I'll show you exactly who I want, Birdie. You're the only one I want around my fingers as you come."

A loud bang of a door closing far away made the air in my throat hitch, and my eyes flew open. Pushing me harder against the wall, his mouth found mine, kissing me hard enough that I forgot where we were. His fingers still working over me.

"Don't pay attention to that. I've got you." His words hot against my ear. "I need you to come on my fingers."

I gasped as he brought me closer to orgasm. I didn't care that it was nearly freezing outside, that we were mere feet away from a busy bar, that, at any moment, someone could walk out and see us standing here. All I needed was his hands on me. His mouth brutal against my own.

As I came, he pulled his kiss away, covering my mouth with his free hand to muffle the cry. His words in my ear as he coaxed me. "That's it. Come all over me. I do this to you. Only me. Those are my fingers inside you, and this is the only cunt they want."

The orgasm washed over me, a sharp heat that crested violently. My nails dug into his biceps, holding me steady against the force. Blood in my ears pounding a beat through me.

Only me.

Only me.

Coming down, sense returned. The rough brick at my back, the nip of cold air, and the...

"Adrian?" A voice broke through the silence. Adrian stiffened, pulling his hand out of my pants. As he turned to face the voice, he did in a way that gave me a minute to put myself together enough to be decent.

"Layla," Adrian said.

My pants zipped, and my sweater adjusted. I was as good as I was going to get after being finger fucked in an alley.

"I was looking for you. My friends are heading over to the other bar, and..."

I stepped out from behind him. Her words faded away. She blinked at me, even in the darkness, her eyes impossibly light. "Oh, you're not alone."

"Hi. Layla, right?" I asked.

"Um, yeah." Layla glanced from Adrian to what had to my wild *I just got my world rocked* hair.

Looping my arm through his, I smiled at her. It was easier to let my jealousy die down after an orgasm. "Adrian mentioned you were a student?"

"A few years ago." Layla's voice faltered.

"That's great. Adrian is so attentive to his kids, isn't he?" I overemphasized the word "kid." Was it mature of me? Absolutely not, but at that moment, I didn't care.

"I guess. It was nice to see you, Adrian. Mr. Winter," she corrected as she turned and left us.

"Feel better now?" he asked me with a smile.

"A smidge," I replied, grinning up at him.

"So, where will you be having your crepes?" he asked.

Wrapping my arms around his waist, I pulled him closer. My words against his mouth. "Your bed. Let's go. We need to make a pit stop first."

CHAPTER TEN

Adrian

FROM THE MOMENT WE went back into the bar to grab out things, I could tell Tam and Penny knew exactly what we had been up to. Thankfully, they didn't say a word to Wren, but I knew from the gleam in their eyes, they'd be talking about this for months.

A quick stop at the store to get supplies, and we were back at the house.

Parking in front of my house, I cut the engine and turned to her. "Stay here."

Condoms in my back pocket, I walked around the back of the truck, opening the door for her but blocking her from getting down. Turning her to face me, her legs on either side of me, she was at my height in her seat. I reached forward, resting my hand on her cheek. "I know we went a little overboard at the bar, but I want to make sure you're comfortable staying over tonight."

"I know." Her response was soft and almost sad. "That's why I want to."

"Should we go inside?" I offered my hand to help her down, and she accepted it.

"I want to go inside, but I have to run over to the house for something. It won't take more than a minute. I'll be right behind you."

I shook my head. "I'll go with you."

Following her to the porch, she opened the door, grabbed a bag from inside, and then turned to me. "I told you one minute."

Grabbing her bag from her hand, I slung it over my shoulder. "Is this an overnight bag? Did you pack an overnight bag for me?"

The color of her cheeks was lovely as she glanced over at me. "It's just a few little things, no big deal."

Smirking, I closed the door behind her, setting the alarm. "Seems like you wanted me to win this bet."

With her hands on her hips, she narrowed her eyes. "The night's not over. I can still decide I want those crepes by myself."

Reaching out, I took her hand, leading her to the steps. From the bottom, we were eye to eye. "You're right, but that leaves a few hours to make sure this is the best night you've ever had."

Her response was to lean forward, taking my mouth with hers in a scorching kiss. My hands wove into her hair as I held her to me. Her legs wrapped around my waist, and through the layers of our winter wear, I could feel the heat of her. Her arm laced around my neck, holding me tight. With a grip on her ass, I walked us across the street and up my front porch.

Breaking the kiss for only a moment to open my front door, her grip on me never wavered. The bag fell from my shoulder, then her purse. A swift kick to the door to slam it shut behind us. I walked across the living room to the bottom of the stairs to my loft bedroom.

I barely registered the clicks of Maizie running around at our feet. Setting her down on the steps above me, I took her face in my hands. "I meant what I said earlier. Don't feel like we have to do anything you don't want to."

"I know exactly what I want." Grasping the bottom of her sweater, she pulled it over her head, flinging it on the floor. Encased in the lacy bra, her tits were firm and high. She ran a hand over her throat and then down her body, stopping at her jeans. Transfixed, I watched her strip tease as she popped the button loose, then the zipper. The jeans slid down to the floor, joining her sweater in a heap to the side. Clad in her bra and thin lace underwear, she turned to walk up the stairs. "You going to join me or stare?"

At the top, I picked her up, tossing her on the bed, where she landed with a soft laugh. Propped up on her elbows, she watched as I took off my sweater, then pants, far less seductively as she did, but I needed to have her skin against mine. Only in my boxers, prowling over her, my mouth found hers. Silky smooth and lush, my hands found her waist, pulling her body flush with mine. My lips roamed from hers to her ear. "You fit so good underneath me."

Her legs wrapped around mine. Two thing pieces of fabric separate us. My cock was hard, rubbing against her. Even through the lace, I knew she was ready for me.

"Are you wet again for me, Birdie?"

"I never stopped." Her nails traced lines on my back. Her hips came up to meet mine, rubbing herself harder against my erection. Groaning, my lips brushed the shell of her ear, her throat, the hollow of her throat. My hands gripped her ass, fitting perfectly in my touch.

"I need all of you." Dipping into the cup of her bra, I pulled out one breast. Taking the pink-brown nipple in my mouth, I made circles with my tongue. My hands behind her, unhooking her bra. Once free, I gave equal attention to her other breast, my thumb pressing and rubbing an equal rhythm to my mouth.

Her hands on my hair, she pressed herself to me. Her moans low and throaty.

Her lacy underwear found themselves on the floor behind me, my touch sweeping over the center of her. Thrusting one finger inside, I found her ready for me, hot and wet.

She let out a low curse at the motion, moving with my hand as I added another finger, curling it in that way I knew she liked. Just as I thought, her body responded to me, flushing across her perfect tits and up her throat.

"I bet you taste better than you feel," I said, plunging back into her dripping pussy.

She ground herself against my palm. "I'm best around your cock."

How I didn't come from those words alone, I had no idea. "Of that, I have no doubt, but I'll have to taste you again to say for certain."

Reaching between us, she pushed down my boxers, freeing my hard cock. Her hand wrapped around the length, pumping it a few times, before I pulled away.

"Not yet. I need you to come first before I fuck you."

One hand splayed over her chest, holding her down against the bed. My mouth reached her mound. Licking over her clit, her fingers tightened in my hair.

"How do you taste better than you did a few hours ago?" I asked. Her response was a low moan as I licked her again, this time sucking her nub into my mouth. I feasted on her, sucking and licking until her cries became louder, her gasps brittle. On each side of my head, her thighs tightened, holding me hostage in the sweetest place. Reaching up, I pinched her nipples, and her back arched. Time dissolved around us. All I had was her body beneath me, the sounds of her cries, and her sweetness on my tongue. There was no desire like this one to stay over her, bringing her closer to the edge. I sucked harder, fucking her with my tongue until she cried out holy names and curses echoing around the room.

Her body loose, falling back against the bed. I pressed a kiss to each side of her inner thigh before covering her body with mine. "Do you need a few minutes?"

Her eyes popped open, a grin on her face. "No, I need more. I need all of you."

I got myself ready, lining up at her entrance. With as much care as I could, I sank into her, her walls tight around me. I wanted to go faster, to spend myself right away, but I had to make this good for her. Once sheathed inside her, I began to move, our bodies coming together. Every thrust, she met. I had never kept my eyes open in sex, but with Wren, I was seeing everything for the first time. The small bite of her lips as I thrust deeper, the way her tits bounced as I pushed inside her. It wasn't just the physical, the gleam of the low light on her skin, the way her hair fanned out against my pillow. She opened her eyes, and for a moment, I couldn't breathe. The deepest look as I took her, communicating something I never knew I wanted before. Deeper and deeper, I was falling into her. I wanted to consume her, to have only that bliss on her face and the sweet moans she made to satiate me.

Her hand came up, cupping my face as I moved inside her. A tenderness cracked inside my chest as we moved together, and I knew there would never be another who would make me feel this way.

Even though she came only minutes before, I knew she was getting closer again. Bending down, I pulled one of her nipples into my mouth, biting down slightly and flicking my tongue over the tip. Her scream of pleasure spurred me on to go faster. Her channel spasmed around me as he fell apart in my arms. One more pump inside her, and I came after her, the pleasure ripping through me with a roar.

Flopping back beside her in bed, I laughed. She glanced over, perplexed. Then she joined me. First, a small chuckle and then we were laughing so hard my sides ached. Yet another first for me. I had fun with sex before, but to lie naked beside someone and find humor in the silence of being wrecked by an orgasm was new.

"That was..."

"Yeah."

Scooping her up, I pulled her flush with my body as we lay on our sides. This kiss was gentle, a brushing of lips. An emotion I couldn't quite identify yet, burrowing in me.

I knew I was going to say the wrong thing, that we only knew each other for a few days, but I couldn't stop the words from coming out. "I didn't know being with a woman could feel this way."

She frowned. "I don't have any right to say this, but I don't want to think about you being with another woman. I got so jealous earlier, and I barely know you."

I argued with myself to tell her that even the sound of her ex's name was sending me into daydreams of doing violent things to a man I envisioned in a pink polo and cargo shorts. "It doesn't feel like we only met a few days ago, does it?"

She laid a hand on my cheek. "How it is between us? I was with another man for years, and he never once touched me the way you do. Not just my body but me."

"Your body, the way your skin flushes for me, those little moans when I've hit the right spot. Nothing will ever compare for me. You are extraordinary."

She ducked her head down, her breathing ragged. "You can't tell me that. This is already complicated enough. I'm leaving in a few days. We shouldn't..."

"What? Get attached?"

Raising her head to gaze at me, she took her lower lip between her teeth. "Something like that."

All this was new ground for me. I had no idea how to handle whatever was growing between us, especially with her leaving. "How do you want to do this?"

A large gulp, then with a shaky breath, she pressed a quick kiss to my lips. "Let's focus on my crepes in the morning, and we can figure out the rest later?"

It was wrong. Despite never being serious about someone, I knew what we had was more than crepes and sex. But to tell her otherwise might cause her to leave. And that was a risk I wouldn't take tonight.

Wren

A snuffling sound woke me as the winter sun filtered odd through the window. I opened one eye to see a small caramel fur face inches from mine. Scrambling into a seated position, the dog sat in her spot between me and Adrian. Her head cocked to the side, she glared at me with an expression of, *What's your damage, lady?*

From the other side of the bed, Adrian slept hard. The white down comforter partially covered his strong lean body. Blinking the sleep from my eyes, I admire the long lines of him, the way his muscled back led down to a shapely ass. The way that ass held firm under my hands the night before as he thrust inside me. One hand was clutching the pillow under his head, the other lazily draped over my legs. His sleeping face lax, he seemed younger than he was at twenty-eight, twenty-nine? Dear Lord, I wasn't even sure I knew his age. Why did I think I could have a fling? Yes, the night before was amazing. Mind-numbing, out of this world, flatten me like a pancake and then give me more, phenomenal. But in the white-and-green light of the morning, all these emotions were mixing around in me. Was this powerful lust and nothing more? Or was something else happening?

Quietly, I moved out of bed, grabbing one of Adrian's discarded shirts off the floor and pulling it on, where it fell to my mid-thigh. That was enough to be decent for a trip downstairs. Tiptoeing down, Maizie followed behind me, her little nails clicking on the hardwood floor.

After a quick freshening up, I saw the towels in his bathroom needed to be refreshed, so I poked around until I found the linen closet. I figured he probably needed the towels washed, so I started a load for him. I picked up the discarded bag off the floor. Then the blankets needed to be folded, so I did that. I saw a few dishes in the sink, so I loaded the dishwasher.

Once I returned the house to a more organized state, I settled on the couch, tucking my knees to my chest. I glanced at my phone, registering today's affirmation, *I use my morning to set goals that bring me closer to achieving my boldest dreams.* Easy for Autumn to say.

Maizie jumped up beside me, her butt wedging between me and the back of the couch. My hand drifted down to her back, petting her while I tried to process my emotions.

This was all getting too complicated. In the countless times I had sex with someone before, I never experienced a moment like last night. With both our eyes open, as we joined together, something shifted inside me. It was one thing to sleep with a man, but the way his eyes softened at me. The sensation of him and I had together was wholly new. How could this man I barely knew make me feel this way? I meant what I said the night before. I was with another man for years, and never had he touched me the way Adrian did.

Shaking my head as if I could dislodge the thought, I focused on what the day would bring. He said he wanted to take me somewhere today. I should do what I said I wanted, focus on having fun, and not think about what the future would hold.

The unknown consumed me. In forty-eight hours, I'd be leaving. This wasn't my home. So, why did I feel so comfortable in his bed? It was a selfish and foolish thing to lie beside Adrian and wish for more. What would happen if I stayed longer?

The floorboard creaked above me, and both Maizie and I glanced over to the stairs to see a shirtless Adrian walk down. Pausing at the foot of the stairs, he ran a hand over his unshaven face. "Hey, ladies."

Maizie sat up straight, her tail wagging as she looked over at her owner. Sauntering over, he leaned down and pressed a quick kiss to my lips before giving the dog a scratch behind her ears.

"I thought we were doing crepes in bed?" he asked.

"You were sleeping so peacefully. I didn't want to disturb you."

He frowned at this but didn't argue. "Let me get you some coffee. Lots of creamer, right?"

I nodded, turning my body on the couch to watch him work in the kitchen. Skillfully, he moved around the room, multitasking breakfast and getting me coffee with ease. As he set the spoon in the sink, he frowned. "Did you wash my dishes for me?"

Heat bloomed over my face. "I put a few things in the dishwasher. I hope that's okay."

With his thumbnail, he scratched at his jaw. "You really don't need to do that for me. You know I can do my own dishes."

"I'm sorry. I shouldn't have overstepped."

Darkness clouded his eyes. "You don't need to be sorry, but I want to be clear here. I can do all those things for myself. I never want you to feel like you have to take care of me, okay?"

"I did it to be nice."

"I see that. But I can and will take care of myself and you, if you'd let me."

Until he said those words, I hadn't realized how much I had fallen into the role of taking care of a man. With Buck, it was assumed I would be cleaning up after us. I was the dishwasher, the laundress, the cleaner. He always said I did it better, that I knew where things went, that it was easier without him in the way to do it wrong.

"I guess it's a habit," I confessed. Tucking my knees closer to my chest, I watched my hand as I pet the back of Maizie's fur.

"I'm not saying I don't appreciate it because I do. But don't do all this because you think I expect it from you. I don't."

What do you expect from me?

No, I couldn't ask that. "It's no big deal." I gave him a smile that, hopefully, reached my eyes.

"Come over here." He motioned me over. Untangling myself from the couch, I set the dog to the side, where she blinked at me, slightly offended by the desertion.

Joining him in the kitchen, he took the half drank coffee from my hands, setting it down on the island behind me.

Running a hand down my arm, he cocked his head to the side. "I could get used to having you here in the mornings."

It doesn't mean anything, Wren. Remember, you're leaving soon. Don't get ahead of yourself.

His hands on my hips, he bent down to press a kiss to my lips. When our mouths touched, an aching formed in my chest at the tenderness of his touch. Our tongues met, and right away, my core heated. The kiss deepened. Our mouths slanted over one another. My hands reached around his back, down the back of his sweatpants to grab his ass and bring him closer.

He pulled away, pointing the spatula at the stool on the other side of the island. "You sit over there, or I'll be ready for round two." He paused, cocking his head to the side. "Or is it three? Anyway, we need to eat before I fuck you again. I have plans that involve you being well fed."

Settling into the stool, I crossed my feet at the ankles and watched as he mixed the batter together. "Plans? Aside from sex?"

He scoffed, the whisk dripping on his wrist as he held it up in mock outrage. "Birdie, there is more to me than my masterful tongue and magnificent cock. I'm a person, you know."

I laughed, taking a sip of my coffee. "So, what kind of non-sex plans do you have?"

He didn't use measuring cups, going by rote memory as he whisked the sugar and flour together. "I didn't say sex was off the table, but I want to take you somewhere."

Narrowing my eyes, I watched him as he poured the batter into the pan. "Where?"

"This little spot at the top of the mountains. The drive is a little bumpy, but the views at the top are incredible." Poking the edges with his spatula, his statement was directed at the pan.

"You want to drive further up a mountain?" I asked skeptically.

He slid the crepe from the pan onto my plate, garnishing it with powdered sugar. "You'll like it. I checked the forecast, and it's supposed to be cold but clear. The views are worth it."

I took a large bite, too ravenous to be dainty. He smiled as I chewed. "Good?"

I gave him a thumbs-up, my mouth too full to respond. As I ate, he started his own batch, cooking quickly. His was far less fancy than the one he gave me, but as he sat beside me, he didn't seem to mind.

"Okay, but promise you won't drive crazy?"

"I would never do anything that puts you in danger. You're safe with me."

I swallowed down the lump that was forming from the simple declaration. I had heard those words before. Most often accompanied by drunken boat rides, where I was whipped about in the cold spray of water. Or the time I got left behind on a double black diamond, my second time snowboarding and had to hike by myself to the lift.

I raised a brow at him. A dull throbbing in my chest at his statement.

"You don't believe me?" he asked, lines forming between his brows. "I would never do something that would make you feel unsafe. I promise."

When I didn't respond, he pushed his half-eaten crepe away from him and turned to face me. "I swear to God. I don't want to hear a thing about your ex because I'd want to slash his tires."

I laughed. Taking the last bite of my food, I licked my fork clean. "He's a non-issue. He dumped me..."

"How that man could be so stupid?"

"He's not stupid. He just didn't want to be with me anymore. I'm okay, I swear."

"It's not okay. You don't have to tell me a thing, and I already know. That man was reckless with you. If I had that kind of chance with you, I'd never be so capricious."

"Look at who's picking up a dictionary to be all swoony."

He leaned forward, his hand on my bare upper thigh. "Is that what gets you going? My big...vocabulary?"

The corner of my mouth ticked up as I leaned in to meet him. "Something like that."

His fingers gripped my chin, bringing me a breath away from his mouth. "You know, when it comes to getting you back in my bed, I plan on being tenacious."

"Who am I to be obstinate?" I murmured. "But who said we need a bed?"

His mouth descended over mine, this time without a hint of tenderness of earlier. His hands found my hips, pulling me into his lap on the stool. The grip on my hips tightened and then his hands were sliding beneath the shirt to grip my ass. My back against the counter, the edge dug into my lower back, but I didn't care. All I knew was the burn of his taste, the rough scrape of his hands as he held tighter. Scooping me up, he hoisted me onto the counter where we were the same height. The embrace deepened, our tongues clashing and teeth knocking. His hands pulled my shirt up and over my head.

"Goddamn, you're bare for me." He leaned back to gaze over my body. The way he was staring at me should have made me self-conscious. Being naked in front of others was never something I enjoyed. All my little and big flaws were on full display in the midmorning light, but all I saw in his eyes was hunger and need.

Slowly, his fingers traced a line down the front of me, between the valley of my breasts, over my soft stomach, and between my thighs to the center of me. "And this pussy is begging to be fucked, isn't it?"

"Why don't you find out?"

He hissed as his fingers dug into my bare hip. Reaching behind him, I pushed his sweatpants down, taking out his hard cock and stroking it.

This time, there was no lengthy foreplay, no tenderness. He drove inside me in a single motion. My head snapped back, hitting the cabinet, but I couldn't register the sting. Wrapping my legs around his waist, I drew him further inside me. His hand laced with my hair. With each thrust inside me, his hand cushioned my head.

"Your cunt fits so good around my cock." He gritted out.

Grabbing his ass, my nails dug into the firm muscles, tightening with each thrust. He would probably have little claw marks on them later, but neither of us cared as he kept ramming into me. The angle of him inside me, paired with his kisses, was sending me closer and closer to climax. The tendons in his neck strained, and I knew he was trying to hold off until I came first.

"Keep fucking me." My heels hooked around each other, my words in his ear. "All I need is this."

In the back of my mind, the clock was ticking. Days—hours, really—left between us and then I would be gone. This was dangerous to allow myself to revel in him. My thoughts must have been all over my face because he pulled back, cupping my face in his hand as continued moving inside me.

"No one else between us."

"No one," I mimed back. The lie I tried to force on myself, that I could be casual, that this was nothing more than a fling, was falling apart faster than I was.

"No one had ever been this good. Your pussy is all I need, Birdie." His words were hot against my ear and then the sharp sting of his teeth on my earlobe. Somehow, that was enough for me. The orgasm hit, cresting over me in wave after wave of white fire.

He followed after me, collapsing against me. His grip on my hips slackened, and his head rested on my shoulder while his breathing steadied. Winding my arms around his middle, I held him close. It was all so familiar, the slickness of our bodies together, the scent of his skin, and the rasp of his beard against my collarbone as I held him tight. To want more of this was foolish, but still, I allowed myself the moment where it could almost be. A world where morning sex and crepes were a constant reality. Where I could hold him tight and know he wanted the same as me. A place where I could belong.

When he pulled away, a soft expression colored his face. His hand came up to cup my cheek. "I wish every morning could be like this."

It could be. Ask me to stay.

I shook my head at the idea. I would never do that. Couldn't. He wasn't the type to want forever. Regaining my composure, I flashed him what I hoped was a convincing grin. "Certainly not my usual wake-up routine."

A dull thud sounded outside, and we both jerked or heads to the side to see a car parked beside Adrian's truck. His grip stilled on my cheek, and the color drained from his face. "Oh, shit."

He pulled away, grabbing the shirt from the floor and tossing it to me. "Quick, put that on."

He pulled the sweatpants up over his still half-hard dick and then held his hands out in front of him as if he could grab a shirt from the air. "Um, um."

He was stuttering.

"What is going on?" I asked, pulling the shirt over my head. He helped me down from the counter, pulling on the bottom of the shirt as if it would go longer than mid-thigh on me.

"It's my parents. What are they doing here? They never come over."

"Your what?" I whisper-shouted, glancing down at myself. I was obviously wearing nothing more than Adrian's old shirt. My hair was likely a wreck of curls, and I was still flushed from my orgasm. "Why didn't you say your parents were coming over?"

"I didn't know." It was too late to do anything but stand there in horror as his parents let themselves into the house.

His mother was first, long, straight ash-blond hair that was obviously professionally highlighted and shaped. She was tall for a woman and slender. Even in the snow, she wore a crisp beige pantsuit and heels. She stopped suddenly at seeing me. His father walked in behind her, almost running into the back of his wife. His father had darker hair, thinning on the top a bit, but a manicured beard. He glanced from me to Adrian with identical blue-green eyes.

"Hi, Mom," Adrian said, his tone level as if he weren't shirtless and standing beside a stranger to them. "Dad."

"Adrian..." His mother cleared her throat. "We were in the neighborhood and..."

She glanced over at her husband with a pleading glance. The man stepped forward, putting his hand out. "Hi there. Gregory Winter, winner of Icicle Creek's best Realtor five years in a row." He put a hand on his wife's back. "This here is Diane, my wife. She is the current champion."

"Oh, please," Adrian cursed, low enough only I could hear it. He cleared his throat. "And my parents. Mom, Dad, this is Wren Alexander."

"Wren?" his mother asked with a raised brow. She took my hand, shaking it with a firm grip. "What an unusual name."

"My mother is very attuned to nature, I guess."

"We seem to have interrupted something." Her eyes darted down to the hem of the shirt on my thighs and Adrian's shirtless chest, then back to my hair.

"Right." I grimaced. "Let me just..." I trailed off, leaving them alone in the living room while I ran up to the loft to find my clothes from the night before. I could hear the indistinct sound of voices but couldn't make out what they were saying. Once dressed, I hesitated at Adrian's dresser. He would need a shirt while talking with his parents. I pulled open the top drawer, grabbing the first tee I saw.

Back in the living room, I handed Adrian the shirt, settling in the spot beside him as he pulled it over his head. Gregory and Diane sat on opposite sides of the larger sofa. The same sofa we had napped the night before after he ate me out on the rug his parents were now stepping on.

"Well, aren't you comfortable with our son?" Diane said, a weak smile on her face.

My eyes snapped to his mother, my reminiscing ending.

"Mom," Adrian warned.

"What?" she asked, putting a square French tip manicured hand to her chest. "It's an observation. We haven't heard from you in weeks, certainly didn't know you were serious about someone, and we show up to say hello and find you here *in flagrante delicto* with this young woman."

Now I know where he gets his air of dramatics.

"It's nothing serious. I'm renting the cabin across the way and..."

"Nothing serious?" Gregory asks with a laugh. "Since my parents passed, Adrian doesn't even like us to come up here, and he's inviting you inside their cabin?"

"Dad," Adrian whispered with urgency.

"What? It's the truth. I know you were close with them, but you moved out of your place in town. You stopped coming to dinner. We barely see you anymore."

Diane turned to face me, a professional smile on her face. "Maybe you can talk Adrian out of this madness. It's not right for a young man to be living all the way out here."

Adrian threw his arm over the back of the couch, his fingers brushing against my shoulder. "It's not that far from town. I love this house, and it's only a ten-minute commute to work. But you don't care about that. Why did you stop by?"

His mother laid a pamphlet on the coffee table. "There's a course coming up in a few weeks. If you study now, you can pass it in no time. We can even pay for the course if you need us to."

"Course?" I asked.

"For his real estate license," Diane explained.

"I have a job."

Gregory sniffed. "That job is thankless, pays crap, and will drive you to gray hairs. You're a smart boy. You should do something more than teach a bunch of fifteen-year-olds about how to conjugate a verb."

"Fifteen-year-olds know how to conjugate verbs," Adrian corrected. "And that's not why I do it. I don't understand why you guys can't leave it alone. I don't care about making a bunch of money."

"Still plenty of time to learn the business. We have a few more years before we retire and…"

"I'm not having this conversation with you guys again. I'm perfectly happy in Gran and Gramps's cabin, being a teacher."

"And sleeping around with tourists?"

"Excuse me?" Adrian raised his voice.

"She is one, right? Wren, you said you are staying in Agatha's cabin? She doesn't live here and has no roots in the community. Just another example of you not taking life seriously."

I sat there, numb, listening to the exchange. Nothing they said was untrue about me, but for them to berate Adrian in front of me was too much. It wasn't my place, but I couldn't listen any longer.

"Excuse me." I stood up, rushing out the side door to stand on the back porch. The icy air was welcome on my scorched face.

Some way to meet his parents.

I couldn't imagine what they would think of me once they got to know me better. If they couldn't respect his job as a teacher, there was no way they would approve of my paltry salary as a data analyst.

Wait, what? They're never going to get to know you. Fling, fling. No future.

A few minutes later, I heard the front door opening and then the starting of the car before it drove away. Adrian walked around the porch, finding me gazing out onto the snow-covered yard.

"They're the worst. I'm sorry they were rude to you."

I shook my head. "I don't care about that. They don't know me. They're going to make assumptions. It was what they said about you that bothered me."

"Me?" He furrowed his brow.

Pushing off from the railing, I turned to face him. "Your parents are supposed to be your biggest supporters. I'm sorry they're hard on you for doing what you obviously love."

"I do." He sighed heavily. "I went into teaching because of my grandparents. They were so proud of me. I can't give it up, even if the pay is crap."

Palm to palm, our fingers laced together. "You shouldn't have to."

Our lips met, and this time, I put all the emotions I couldn't quite say into my kiss. His arms wrapped around my waist, pulling me closer. When he pulled away, there was a heaviness in his eyes, as if he wanted to say something serious. His thumb traced over my bottom lip, and I gently kissed the pad of his thumb. "I..."

In the back of my head, the alarm bells were ringing.

You're leaving in two days. What do you expect this man to do?

Covering his hand with my own, I stared up at him, willing him to ask me to stay longer, to be more.

Blinking several times, his eyes cleared. "We should get going. We're wasting good daylight."

Adrian

TRULY, I COULDN'T HELP but wonder how I ever sprang from my parents. Once the embarrassment of them bursting into my place and almost catching Wren and I was over, all I felt was annoyed. It was the same conversations we always had: lost potential, wayward priorities, and a dash of condescension.

But the way they spoke to Wren was too much. Ordinarily, I would have let them ramble on, saying whatever it took to get them out, but for them to talk to Wren as if she was some random woman I brought home and not... Well, I hadn't quite figured out what Wren was to me. All I knew was she was more. And to have my parents with their crisp suits and disdainful glances was a hurdle I hadn't foreseen.

As we ascended the old logging road up the mountain, I closed up the box in my head where my parent's words echoed around.

"You're not serious about anything, almost thirty, and can't even settle down. Do you even know how to be in a relationship?"

I didn't. All my life, I'd seen examples of what being part of a couple would be, but had I ever put these theories into practice? No. And my parents, of course, cut to the quick to name all my flaws. I didn't need them to tell me I was stunted in this area. To conflate my lack of relationships with what they considered my meandering existence.

Locked up tight in the box in my brain, I made the left turn at the fork that would lead us to the top. The truck bumped along the gravel switchback road up the mountain. At one point, I glanced over to see Wren gripping what my friends and I always called the "oh-shit handle" and grimacing at each bump.

"I've been driving this road since I was sixteen. It's safe, I promise."

Her eyes darted to me and then quickly back to the road. "Are you sure?"

I reached over, setting a hand on my leg and squeezing it. "I am."

"Both hands on the wheel!" she barked.

Dutifully, I complied, chuckling at her response.

We passed the sledding hill, where children in puffy snowsuits were dragging brightly colored plastic sleds up the small hill. Their parents crowded around a small fire with mugs in their hands.

She leaned forward, watching as the kids squeezed into the sleds, their limbs piled on top of each other before they slid down the hill with shrieks and laughter.

Sticking my hand out the window, I waved to the parents, who waved back.

"Do you know them?" Wren asked.

Shaking my head, I pushed the button on the dashboard to switch my truck to four-high. "No."

"But you waved at them."

"It's mountain courtesy."

She repeated my words back to me with a raised brow. "Yeah, acknowledging other people, saying hello. We all share the mountain here." Seeing her confused expression, I went on. "Is that not normal?"

With a sigh, she rubbed her hands together. "I'm starting to think I don't know what normal behavior is. Or common courtesy, for that matter. It's like I was in a fog, not realizing how warped my world had been for so many years." She glanced over at me. "Sorry, I shouldn't be unloading on you like that."

I reached over, taking her hand in mine. "It's fine. I want to know about you."

She squeezed my hands once before throwing it back at me, pointing at the steering wheel. Smiling, I gripped the wheel tightly and increased the speed as we took the narrow hill up the top. On the passenger side, the treetops gave way to an open valley below as the edge of the road dropped away.

"Geez! Could you maybe not go fast?" she asked, then a darkness clouded her features, and she glanced at me with a furrowed brow. "It's just that I'm a little freaked out by the cliffs on the sides, and I know you said that you've been driving these roads since you were young, but I've never done this and..."

"Hey, of course I will." Slowly applying the brakes, my speed decreased. It wasn't as fast as I enjoyed going, but her white-knuckling it as we went through the curves wasn't an option.

Clearing her throat, she glanced away. "Thank you. I know you probably think I'm being dramatic, and I hate to put a damper on your fun in the snow..."

"I'm glad you told me. It's not fun if you don't feel safe."

Her big brown eyes blinked at me, almost glossy. She couldn't be crying over that, right? "Are you sure? I don't want to be one of those bummer girls who can't take risks and hold you back."

Bummer girls. The idea was preposterous. Was that what she thought of herself as? A darkness rolled in my gut at her words. Having her think she couldn't tell me if she was uncomfortable or scared because she didn't want to bother me was terrifying. Is this how she lived?

"You wouldn't be holding me back. I'm glad you told me. I care about how you feel. You can tell me no. You could have said you didn't want to come up this mountain. We can turn around right now and go back down. Whatever makes you comfortable. It won't change my opinion of you."

"Bet?" she asked softly.

"Bet." I agreed.

Nothing you say could change how I'm feeling about you.

I blinked away the thought. It was far too soon to put into words what was happening between us. I barely knew her. No, that wasn't entirely true. I did know her. Maybe not the specifics, like her favorite book, or the name of her second-grade teacher. But we knew each other in a way, recognized something in one another, that no amount of time together could force.

A break in the trees and then the space opened before us. Pulling off the road, I parked in the clearing facing the west. From the high elevation, we could see the thin line of Vancouver, Canada, on the other side of the Strait of Juan de Fuca.

Wren got out, her arms crossed over her chest as she took in the view. "Oh, wow," she whispered. She glanced back at me. "This is incredible."

My arms wrapped around her, pulling her back to my chest. I rested my chin on the top of her head. "Worth the wild drive?"

Turning her head, she gave me a devious grin. "Almost. I think I'll need a little more to be persuaded."

I smirked at her, bending low until my mouth was almost on hers. "What kind of persuading?"

My mouth slanting over hers, we met. The slight wind picked up little shards of snow swirling around us and biting at our cheeks. With her in my arms, I couldn't feel the cold. The kiss turned into more, and she twisted to face me, her arms wrapping around my waist to pull me closer. Backing her into the side of my truck, the embrace became crushing. A lust pounding through me as I wanted to strip her bare and have my way with her on this mountainside. She gripped the zipper on my jacket, to pull it down, making it halfway before I pulled back. "Wait. Not yet."

She dropped the zipper, and I stepped back to give her space. "I didn't bring you up here for that."

With an arched brow and a smirk, she looked me up and down. "No?"

"Not only that. I really did want you to see the views here." I never had the urge to take a woman to this spot before, but I wanted Wren to see the best of the area. The best of me. While I was still unsure how to proceed with whatever it was that was building between us, I knew I wanted to share this special place with her. I might not be able to these growing emotions into words, but I had the wide expanse of trees and the gray-blue waters that led to the ocean. I had the trees and the amber and gray rocks that had been my childhood.

Unlocking my tailgate, I grabbed her by her waist, hoisting her up on the back. Her legs dangled over the edge as I hopped beside her. With the well-loved thermos of hot chocolate at my side, I poured her a small mug and then myself one. Together we sat in an easy silence, the winter air cold and biting our cheeks but the hot drink warming us. "As a kid, my Gramps would take me up here for sledding, like those kids we passed. I thought, for years, we were the only ones in the world to know about that spot, but once I grew old enough to drive, I realized a lot of people know about it." I pointed down a narrow road to the left. "And over there. My grandparents used to bring me up here every December. We'd pick out a tree for the cabin and cut it down ourselves."

"You can do that. Cut down whatever tree you want?"

I laughed. "No, you buy a pass at the ranger station. My parents have this beautiful fake tree they bought years ago, but coming out here with my grandparents always meant more to me. Even when the tree we picked was lopsided or five feet too tall. Somehow, it was better in my mind than this perfectly symmetrical thing my parents decorated with all white and silver baubles.”

Wren scrunched her nose and gritted her teeth. “Yeah, I can see how your parents might be like that. No offense. I’m sure their home is lovely during the holidays, though.”

I laughed. “None taken, trust me. And it is gorgeous and cold. When I was little, they’d let me put my kid ornaments low on the tree, but as I got older, they were left in the box. But my grandparents always let me put whatever I wanted on the tree. Broken popsicle stick reindeer and chipped clay candy canes. If I made it, they wanted it.”

“You miss them a lot, don’t you?” she asked.

“Every day.” My words were honest, but for the first time, I didn’t feel saddened by them. “They would have liked you. My Gramps would have said you were a looker.”

“A looker?” She smiled at the description.

“And my Gran would have told me my picker was finally working. She said I had a broken picker if I couldn’t find the right girl.”

Our eyes met, and it was as if the cold vanished. The icy wind fell away, and all I had was the warmth of her topaz eyes on me, the deep sincerity in her expression. Never had the urge to fall into someone come on so suddenly. The long moment stretched on, unspoken and fierce. I leaned forward at the same time as her satellites to one another. Suddenly, she reared back, shaking her hand. Hot chocolate had sloshed over the rim of her mug, over her hand.

“You okay?” I asked, concern lacing my words as I took the hot chocolate from her and inspected her hand.

“Yeah, it’s not that hot anymore.”

The moment between us broke, her eyes cut away from mine. Staring across the far reach of the skyline, she pointed to the north. “What is that over there?”

Narrowing my eyes, I looked. "That's Vancouver Island."

"Canada?" She raised a brow.

"Yep, Canada. When I was little, my parents would take me on the Black Ball Ferry up to Victoria once a year. We'd stay at the Grand Pacific across from the ferry terminal. Go to the wax museum and Butchart Gardens. Be real tourists."

"I've never been to Canada," she mused, her eyes growing soft as she gazed out over the scenery. She opened her mouth as if to say something and let out a hard sigh. Shaking her head, her eyes darted down to her boots. "My mom isn't allowed. Actually, she got arrested in 1994 for drug possession with intent to sell."

"Wait, seriously?"

She nodded, letting out a low, humorless chuckle. "Yeah, it was before I was born, obviously. But she was dating some guy and made some mistakes. She didn't do much time, but it was still a felony on her record. She had a hard time finding work. We moved around a lot, sometimes multiple times in a year when my parents could find work."

"That's tough," I ventured.

"Nah, it was okay. I mean, sure, my mom can never work in health care or education or law enforcement, or, well, you get the idea. But my dad had a good enough job, and we were finally able to settle down when I was seventeen in Ridgewood. Though we never could go to Canada."

I'll take you.

Her gaze far away, she kept talking, opening up to me. "My parents, they thought the constant moving around was an adventure."

"Not quite for you, though," I ventured.

Shaking her head, she spared me a quick glance. "I would have loved coming up to the same spot for a Christmas tree every year. Having the same table to eat family dinners. I think..." She paused, her cheeks flooding. "I think that maybe that's why I held on so long with Buck. Because at least he was consistent. His family had heirlooms, and his mom would invite me over for Thanksgiving and Easter dinner. For a while, it was nice being around someone who had traditions. But in the end, it wasn't enough to stay."

"No, it's not." With exactly zero experience in long-term relationships, I still knew the answer.

Tucking her hands under her legs, she frowned. "I don't know if I even know what a good relationship looks like."

"I do," I replied. And I told her. About my grandparents, their commitment to each other, from their first meeting to the years together. The way my Gramps always filled her car with gas without being asked or the way my Gran would bring his coffee every morning while he was getting ready for the day.

Wren's eyes grew glossy with warmth. "That is so romantic."

"I always thought that idea was a fluke thing. Only reserved for people like my grandparents, but now, I'm not so sure."

"Are you saying you believe in love at first sight?" she asked, laughing softly.

I cleared my throat. "I'm saying, sometimes, when we meet someone, if we're really lucky, we can know they hold the possibility of more."

"That sounds like attraction and lust," she corrected.

"Maybe, but it's still there. The way someone could burst into your life, and deep down, you know nothing will ever be the same, and you can't explain it or rationalize it. You just want."

"You want," she repeated back to me, her voice struggling to sound incredulous. I had the distinct impression she was fighting something inside her at my words.

"I want."

Her breath shaky, she covered her mouth, giving a wavering laugh into her palm. "I don't know what to think when I'm around you. If I was making a bet, I would have never guessed that you'd say that."

"I'm going on three oh with our bets. Are you sure you want to keep gambling with me?"

"Maybe I'm letting you win." She countered. "What if I'm a dark horse ready to claim the top prize? Waiting for you to put down your defenses before I ride to victory."

"Who says you haven't already knocked my defenses down?"

She sobered. "Have I?"

I leaned back, not wanting to look at her as I said the words. "If you had asked me a week ago, I would have told you I was fine. But now, spending time with you. I'm not so sure. Something about you. About us together, makes me realize how much was missing from my life."

Beside me, she sucked in a breath.

"There you go, being suave again."

"It's not me trying to be suave, it's sincerity."

She crossed her arms against her chest as if to keep herself together. "How could I know that?"

I fought back the lump of annoyance at her statement. She had been hurt. Her honesty was one of the many things I appreciated about her. So, why would I expect her to trust me when I said I wouldn't do the same? It might take weeks, months, or years before she would realize that my words were true. I realized with a start that I would give her that. If she wanted it, I would give her the time. I'd show her I meant every word.

"Because I know this is too soon, and I know I was running my mouth a few minutes ago, but I meant every word. And right now, those words say that I desperately want to kiss you."

This kiss was blistering—no slow pecks and warning caresses. One moment, I'm sitting beside her, the next, she's flat on my back, my body pinning her to the bed of the truck. The cold air whipped around us, but I could barely feel it with her hands reaching into my coat and my lips on her throat.

The kiss lasted only a minute when she pulled away, holding my face in her hands. "As much fun as this is, I don't want to chance hypothermia for the second time in two days."

I pulled away, rolling off her. She hopped down from the truck, walked to the driver's side, and opened the door. "Get in."

"You ready to head back?" Trying to keep the disappointment out of my voice, I adjusted my hard-on in my pants. My erection would have to wait until we got back to the cabin.

She gave me a wicked grin. "I'm ready for a ride, but we're not going anywhere."

I'm surprised I didn't fall off the tailgate as I stumbled down.

Wren

I T WAS A TIGHT squeeze in the front seat. He made quick work of his coat, pants, and shirt. I climbed into the passenger seat, stripping down to my underwear.

Desperate times call for horny measures. Shucking my jeans and sweater, I fling them into the back seat.

We meet in the middle over the console, clashing tongues and hands roaming over each other's bodies. I haven't made out in a car since I was in high school, and the thrill of it hasn't abated. Adrian reaches into my underwear, his fingers delve inside me as his thumb presses firmly against my clit, the pressure sending sparks through me.

"Such a greedy cunt," he growled as he added another finger. "So wet and ready. Did you feel empty without me? Tell me, Birdie, what would make you whole?"

I gasped as his thumb pressed harder on my clit. "You."

"My what? My hands, my mouth?" His dirty words beat a steady rhythm inside me. "Tell me, and I'll give it to you."

"Your cock. I need your cock inside me." I pushed hard against his chest with one hand, while taking out his hard cock with the other. It was an awkward climb over the middle console, but I did it. My legs were now on each side of his hips. I grabbed his hair, pulling his face to mine for a kiss. His cock rubbed against my bare cleft.

His hands reached behind me, unhooking my bra. It fell away somewhere on the floor. His mouth found my nipples, sucking one into his mouth while he played with the other. My back arched to the sensation, hitting the steering wheel. A loud honk sounded, startling us both. The echo of it going through the mountain valley for a long minute.

I opened my mouth to apologize, and it came out as a laugh. He joined in, the low deep rumble in his chest shaking us both. Despite the funny moment, the motion also sent a vibration to my core.

Rubbing my slick heat against his cock, I bent down inches from his lips. "Sorry if I killed the mood."

"You didn't kill a thing." His eyes dark with lust again. "If anything, it makes me want to sink even deeper into you."

In a mess of limbs, we were able to find a condom. I slid it down his length, not bothering with being sultry. The need to have him inside me is overwhelming. He was right. I was empty without him. My fist pumped up and down his cock before I pulled myself up, lining him up with my entrance. With my hands on his shoulders, I slowly lowered myself onto him. His thick cock stretching me as he went deeper. I hissed as I took him. His hands on my hips, not controlling the speed but holding on tight as I took him.

"You're so fucking tight for me, Birdie."

He had felt big the night before, but this angle, the way I held him inside me, hit spots I didn't know were erogenous.

As I rose above him, he reached up to grab a hold of the nape of my neck. The sting of him pulling my hair as he tilted my head up to suck on my neck. Between the scrap of his teeth against the tender flesh, and the slap of my ass hitting his legs, I rode him hard.

"That's it, use me," he gritted out between clenched teeth. "Fuck it out of me."

The tempo picked up, and I chased my pleasure. I had been on top during sex before but never like this. His hands on me were strong, but I was the one in control. The power of holding both our pleasures between my thighs taking me higher. No one had ever given themselves over to me in this way before, and in that, I was able to give myself as well.

"Let go," he crooned as I held tight to his shoulders. "Give it all to me."

The waves wouldn't come. Something dark was holding me back. He captured my mouth, with his lips firm and brutal against my own. Our tongues lashed at each other as he continues to move inside me. I brought myself up his shaft to slam back down. His groan was hot against my neck. I needed something more, but I didn't know what it was. His grip was tight on my hips, and I leaned back to watch his face as I moved above him.

A tendril of my hair came loose, but he tucked it behind my ear. His hand gripped the back of my neck as he watched me. "I want to keep you. Tell me you're mine," he whispered.

The tiny fissures that had been splitting since that first night cracked into shards. I knew I couldn't stay. This was never supposed to come with possession. But here we were. I wanted to own him, to keep every inch of his skin to myself. There was no stopping the insidious need inside me to respond. "I'm yours, and you're mine."

"You will always have me." His words were harsh but honest. "This between us is precious, you understand. I'm never going to want anyone else."

Those words flooded through me, breaking me wide open. A ruthless need to be claimed by him in a way I never had before.

"Prove it," I said, edging him closer to climax. "Show me."

With a violent gleam in his eye, he pulled my hair harder, my neck tilting back. His mouth was on my breast, his teeth scraping the skin around my nipple. The sting was good until it was searing. His bite harsh and painful, but instead of pulling away, I rocked faster against him, driving each of us closer. His tongue lashed out on the stinging flash he bit, licking and sucking. I was going to bruise, to scar, and I didn't care.

"If I could tattoo my bite into your skin, I would. I want the world to know exactly who this body belongs to."

"It's yours."

He gave me a knowing smirk as he slid his hand between us to rub my clit.

With his mouth on my breast and his hand on my clit, I arched my back, sliding into him one last shuddering time. The climax was a blinding heat behind my eyes as I cried out.

"That's it. Show me how my Birdie comes all over my cock," he growled. The tendons in his neck stood out as he came right after me.

My breathing shaky, I collapsed against him, my face buried in his neck. The slickness of our sweat and the heat of our bodies made the air in the cabin thick. I inhaled the woodsy scent of him, all clean and masculine.

As the lustful haze fell from my eyes, I considered the words we said to each other. Platitudes and terms of endearment were practically meaningless in the heat of sex. So, why did everything I said feel so true? An overwhelming urge to cry thundered through me. If we could have stayed there, in that cramped front seat, nothing but the snow-capped mountains and the slick of our skin together, I would have. But it wasn't real. We couldn't be. He wasn't the type to want more, and I was a total mess and a half. In what world could this ever be more?

Pulling myself up, I moved to get off him, and he stopped me. His hand cupped my cheek, his thumb tracing over my bottom lip. Our eyes caught on each other, and as I peered down at him, a vulnerability in his gaze had me even more raw.

This was supposed to be sex—fun and casual and not at all the lead-up to emotional tragedy.

"I said too much, didn't I?" he asked softly.

I shook my head, half believing in the motion. His words were overwhelming but not in the way he was worried about. I wanted them too much, craved the little ember that was burning brighter inside my chest. I had been told forever before but never like this. If I felt this way today, how would it be in a few days, when I left Adrian behind?

"You said all the right words. Everything from the moment I met you has been exactly right. That's what's making this all so hard. In less than forty-eight hours, I'll be gone."

Blackness clouded over his features at the mention, but there was no getting around it. Once we left this mountain, we had one more night together and then the real world was returning.

"I don't expect anything of you, I swear." I laid a hand on his chest, reassuring him of that. Did I want more? Of course. But to ask for it? To believe that we could be anyone but who we are, was a foolish idea.

We made no plans, there were no declarations. I couldn't hope for something that wouldn't work outside our bubble. He had a job he went back to after the mid-winter break. I had—well, okay, nothing was keeping me at my parents' house. But what kind of person would I be to stay here with Adrian if he didn't want me to?

"Right. Forty-eight hours," he echoed, his voice flat. "We'll have to make them count."

He let go of his grip on my hips, letting me climb back over the console and grab our clothes from their various places strewn around the inside of the truck. Once dressed, the silence between us was thick. The click of the key in the ignition and Adrian's hand behind my head as he backed up.

On the other side of the road, the cliff side edge didn't seem as daunting as we made our descent. The radio was nothing but static. Bringing up how much time I had left was a mistake. Now he was probably worried I was vying for a commitment from him.

I hated long awkward silences, always had. Even when I knew the smart choice would be to not say anything, my mouth opened, and out came ridiculous words. "You know, next time, we'll have to go in the back seat. It looks a little roomier."

"Next time?" A small smile quirked on the corner of his mouth. "How many times do you plan on having sex in my truck?"

"How many times will you let me?" I asked back, giving me a casual smirk. The question was far more loaded than I wanted to admit, but I hoped my tone was casual.

I can be cool. I can be fun.

"I'll pull the truck over right now for a round two." He mimed jerking the steering wheel to the side, and I laughed.

"I bet you say that to all the girls."

"What girls? Before you, I've never defiled my truck with sex before."

"Defiled?" I slapped a hand over my heart. "Is that what you call what we did?"

He glanced over at me, his eyes that earnest blue green. "No, what we had was consecrated."

The thump of my heart was ringing in my ears, my chest suddenly too tight. How could he say these things so easily?

"Well, I might have thrown in a few holy names in the throes of passion," I admitted.

This time, when he reached over to take my hand, the tension was gone.

Halfway down the mountain, we passed a truck in the ditch; the back tires lifted in the air, and the front tires spun useless against the snow and gravel mixture. Apparently, this was a common enough thing because Adrian let out a low chuckle and pulled to the side to park beside them. Two young boys emerged from the old SUV, red-faced and frowning.

With a squeeze to my thigh and the promise that I'd stay in the truck to stay warm, Adrian climbed out.

They must have been students of his because both boys visibly relaxed when they saw Adrian shaking his hand. On my knees, I twisted in the seat to watch as Adrian and the two teens assessed the situation, gesturing and laughing. The blond one pantomimed what must have been the moments before they hit the ditch. After a few minutes of talking, Adrian shook his head at them, frowning, and then went to the bed of his truck to retrieve a chain.

He directed the boys to various spots, pointing out where they needed to be and how they could help him. First, he crouched down below the tailgate of their truck, attaching the tow rope to something I couldn't see. Then he popped back up to attach the other side to his own truck. The truck swayed and moved as he jerked the pieces into place.

When he saw me standing outside the truck, he frowned. "You don't have to wait out here. It's warmer in the truck."

If he was working in the cold, it was silly for me to sit in front of the warm heater and watch from the safety of his leather seats. "It's okay. I don't mind."

That got me an incredulous glare, but he didn't argue.

"I didn't know Mr. Winter was married," the dark-haired one said.

Damn, it was cold out here. My coat was warm, but the icy sting of the snow kicking up from the ground was enough on my cheeks. "He's not."

The kid blinked, assessing me. Obviously, this kid was old enough to drive, at least sixteen, but that didn't make him that much younger than me. I could have been his older sister. A brief glimpse of how weird it must be for Adrian to teach people, some only ten years younger than him, must be.

"Oh, so you're, like, his girl?"

Teenagers were not my thing. I wasn't even sure I liked them when I was one. Small children, sure, babies, give me their chubby little tummies and squishy cheeks. These kids, taller than me but missing half a prefrontal cortex. No, thank you.

"We're friends."

The kid laughed. "Glad to hear Mr. Winter's getting it. Didn't know Teach had the skills to snag like that."

Incessantly blinking with a frown, I tried to decipher his words. Opening my mouth to respond with...what? No clue, honestly, when Adrian walked up, slapping his hands together in their thick leather gloves.

"Okay, hop back in, Birdie. I'll tow them out."

Once he was sure all the items were safely attached, he motioned for me to get back in the truck. He told the boys to put the truck in neutral.

Bits of snow and dirt clung to his jacket as he climbed back into the truck. A swipe of mud or possibly grease on his forehead and into his hair. His jacket had damp spots and what was likely a stain blooming across the side.

Shifting into reverse, we drove back a few feet, and then the truck stopped moving or a minute. Our tires spinning, neither truck was moving now. He cursed low, getting out and slamming the door. An exaggerated gesture and a yell about the brakes being on and then he was back in the truck. This time, both of the vehicles moved. It wrenched the small older truck violently back onto the road, and all four tires now firmly on the gravel and snow road.

"Stay here." He reached over and tightened my seatbelt as if I were about to fly away.

"You got it, *Teach*."

As he climbed out, I heard a low mumble of how I deserved a spanking. A big grin on my face. I watched as he unhooked everything.

The teenager's truck now firmly on solid ground, the boys got out smiling. "Thank you, Mr. Winter. We owe you one."

The glower he gave the boys could only be described as a veteran teacher about to lay down the law. "I want you boys to go back down the mountain. No more donuts in the snow without proper tools."

"Sure thing, Teach." One of the boys saluted.

"And dump out that beer. I don't know whose basement mini fridge you stole this swill out of, but I'm not letting you drive a yard down the road until it's in the ditch."

"Oh, come on, man! Weren't you ever a kid wanting to have some fun?" the dark-haired boy asked.

"It's just light beer," the other boy chimed in. "Practically water."

"Out." Adrian pointed to the ditch. The boys grumbled a bit longer before grabbing the beer and cracking each can. The yellow liquid splashed over the grimy snow of the ditch.

"I'm going to be following you down the mountain, so no side trip until we get to the highway, got it?"

Contritely, the boys climbed into their truck, making their way down the snow-covered road.

Once we were safely in the truck behind them, Adrian started the descent.

"Dumb kids." He shook his head. "Not dumb but no sense. Coming up here in a two-wheel-drive truck with no tow rope, no spare water—unless you count a six-pack of light beer and not even a wrench between them."

As if I could understand half of what he said, I nodded. "Yeah, wild."

The chagrined look he flashed me had me smiling bigger. "If I hadn't come by, I have no idea how they would've gotten out."

"Did you really need to make them dump out their beer?" I asked.

From his spot in the driver's seat, Adrian flashed me a grin. "Nah, probably not. I could have pretended it didn't see it under the old sweatshirt they threw on top, but honestly, messing with kids is so much fun I couldn't help it."

"You could have taken the beer and drank it. That's what my parent's friend did when she caught me drinking with my friends as a teen."

Scrunching up his nose. "Free beer is my favorite beer, but even I have to draw the line somewhere. That stuff tastes like a moldy sweat sock soaked in lime juice."

"Had a lot of experience with moldy sweat socks?"

Reaching across the console, he grabbed my side, squeezing my ribs. With it being the most ticklish spot on my body, I squirmed away. "No tickling the Birdie."

"It's not a tickle. It's a massage." His hand moved down to my knee, squeezing that. I let out a snort and kicked my leg.

"No massage," I shrieked out between fits of laughter, trying to push his hand away. "Hands on the wheel, Mr. Winter."

His straight white teeth flashed as he removed his hands from me. "Okay, fine. But now that I know all your weak spots, I might need to exploit them later."

"Is that a threat?" I asked in mock outrage.

"A promise."

As the gravel road gave way to pavement and the lanes widened, I knew we were getting closer to the cabins. The clock was ticking between us. I had two more nights. The sun was setting behind the oversized cedars. One more full day with him.

And then it was back to my parents' empty house. To seeing familiar faces on the street and having nothing at all to report when asked, *What have you been up to?*

Back to a place where I had nothing waiting for me.

Adrian

B ETWEEN DINNER AND SEX on the couch and then dessert and me going down on her the kitchen floor, the night was a success. We drank a bottle and a half of wine before we headed up to the bedroom, our clothes discarded in various spots around the cabin.

While most of my experiences were one-night only interludes, I had a few flings with women. Long weekends, where we stayed together and had sex all over the place in their rented condos or vacation homes.

At the end of the long weekends, I was ready to leave. Ready to return to my life.

Not with Wren. Every time with her opened up new sensations. I got to learn her body. The way she liked it when I scraped my teeth against her skin or the little mew of pleasure she let out the first time I entered her. Responsive in my hands, my need for her grew, not decreased. How could one weekend ever be enough?

She needed to stay with me. I wanted her beside me in a desperate way. I had never wanted another person.

As a child, I got up in the middle of the night a lot. I would wander around the house. The stillness of my parents' large home, cold and forbidding. I'd go into their office and touch their leather chairs, the blotter under each of their keyboards, and flip through their Rolodex filled with important phone numbers of important people. This office that they spend hours in. The office I was supposed to take over some day.

I wish I was important enough to be seen by them for who I was. I knew they loved me in an off-hand way, more like a precious pet. They showed up for the important stuff, but it all felt for show. Back at home, it was their office, their den, with their cocktails.

Tam would complain to me about his parents making him go on long road trips with his family. Places like Yellowstone, Fairmont Hot Springs, and The Badlands.

My parents would take me to five-star resorts in tropical locales, leaving me in the kids' club while they would sun by the pool.

Tam would complain, but he had inside jokes with his family about the time his sister ate a whole can of Pringles in five minutes. Or when his brother joked to a border agent that his parents weren't actually his parents. An easy camaraderie that I would never have. I didn't want to want those things. But sometimes, I wondered.

"Tell me about your home?" I asked.

Wrinkling her nose, she considered the question. "Ridgewood? It's okay, I guess. It's the closest thing I had to a hometown, but it's never really felt like it to me. Maybe it's because I only have a few friends I still talk to from school. It's a beautiful place on the water, and they have adorable touristy stores on Front Street and a great bakery that makes these huge donuts shaped like a person, doughboys."

"I like donuts."

"But I always felt like a tourist there. Never a resident, never a home. My mom used to tell me I needed to bloom where you're planted. Something she read on the front of a Mary Engelbreit card, I suspect. But to use a flowery analogy, it's not that simple. Flowers don't bloom wherever they are planted. It takes a myriad of factors, sunlight, soil pH, amount of water, and seasons. To plant one without care will only cause it to wilt and die." She ducked her head, her cheeks coloring. "That's a terrible analogy."

"No, it's not. I get it. Certain flowers can spring up between sidewalk cracks, but you—that's not you. For someone like you, it takes more to bloom."

She nodded slowly.

I didn't want to be happy about her not feeling like she had a home. It was a terrible thing, but selfishly, I reveled in it. If she had no home in Ridgewood, maybe I could be her home—maybe... I sighed. What was I thinking? It was too soon, too fast. I was being foolish.

"So, what's your plan now?"

With a glance away, she chewed on her bottom lip. "I don't know. I've never been able to put down roots before. Sorry for the plant pun again. With the person not to be named, I was going along with what he wanted to do. He wanted to live in Seattle, so we did. He wanted me to be home for him, so I got a job that worked from home. But now, I don't know where to go or what to do."

Stay here with me, I thought. But I couldn't say that. It was too soon. She was still hung up on the ex, no matter what she said. I had no idea how to be there for someone else. My grandparents had taken care of me, while my parents ignored and chided me. What were the first steps in commitment? How do you know when it's right?

How could I give Wren what she needed when I wasn't sure was capable of that in the first place? A weekend of sex and pretty words weren't enough. Even I knew that. I saw what other people had, and as much as I wanted that with Wren, the words to get there. The actions felt so far away.

The clock was ticking faster on us. She had nothing to stay for if I didn't ask her, but how do you say those words?

Holding her closer in bed that night, I told myself the next morning we would talk. Surely, there was an option where we could see each other again? I could visit her, and she could visit me, and eventually, we'd...what? A momentary gasp of panic seized me. What were the steps, move in, marriage, kids? Is this what you did when you cared for someone?

It wasn't a panic because I could picture it. All too easily, the images flooded my mind. The way she might redecorate the cabin. A small ceremony at the riverside and a reception at the diner. The way my old room could be turned into a nursery.

These ideas came unbidden and strong. I could picture myself with Wren. From the moment I saw her on my front porch, it was exactly as my grandfather had explained it. There would never be another for me. There was never a serious girlfriend before her because the universe knew all I would need was her. Would I be enough for her? Could I be her home?

Eyes drifting shut, I knew tomorrow would change what we had from a fling to something else.

CHAPTER FIFTEEN

Wren

THE NIGHT WAS PERFECT. The sleep was perfect, and the waking beside Adrian was more than perfect. I watched the rise and fall of his chest as he slept. The thin dusting of golden-brown hair on his pecs, the small birthmark under his jawline, the perfect size for kissing. Maizie joined us, once again, snuggling between our legs and snoring softly as if this were the most natural place in the world.

And it was. For years, I would wake before Buck and fix my hair, brush my teeth, wipe off the smudges of mascara beneath my eyes. All so he wouldn't see that side of me. Sleeping beside Adrian, my hair in its bonnet, no makeup on, my mouth stale, I felt safe. Across Adrian's cheek was a pillow crease, going from his ear to the corner of his mouth. Softly, I ran a finger down it, soothing the spot. The bristle of his unshaven cheek was rough against my finger, and I reveled in the soft glow of the white morning light across our naked bodies.

We're like a picture. Lovers embraced.

Two lovers entwined. The lazy way his arm was over my waist, the dog curled up alongside us, the tangle of limbs. I felt like art. What was growing between us, how I was feeling, was a beautiful ache.

I wanted him. I wanted this. The logistics of how we could work were nagging in the back of my mind. Where would I stay? I couldn't just move here after a long weekend together, could I? As lovely as the words Adrian said to me, there was no promise in them. He didn't ask me to stay. If there was one thing I learned from my fiasco of a relationship with Buck, it was that I would never expect more than I was being offered.

I wasn't going to ask Adrian. This was his world, his town. I was a visitor to it. Only he could decide if he wanted me to stay.

Beside me, Adrian stirred, his large hand flexing on my hip, then moving down to grasp my ass. He mumbled contentedly, pulling me closer.

"My kind of wake-up," he said, his voice still sleep-tinged. Ordinarily, I'd be concerned about morning breath, but when he leaned over to kiss me, I relaxed in his embrace. Soon, the covers were pushed to the side, the condom was on, and he was inside me. Even sleepy, he was masterful, his touch sending sparks of awareness through me.

This is how it should be. This is how it could be.

We came together, him finding his release moments after me. When he collapsed on top of me, his head nestled between my neck and my shoulder. "I take it back. That is my kind of wake-up."

His smile is so bright, so earnest. It felt like a balloon was inside my chest, about to pop. My breath shaky, I took his mouth, kissing him again. He rolled off me, pulling me to lie beside him. My head on his chest, his hand in my hair, gently combing.

"After my mother's comment about your name, I looked it up. I've never been an animal guy, so I wasn't even sure I knew what a wren was."

"It's a small brown bird. Known to be loud and bold."

"The small part is right, but I don't think you're very loud or bold."

I have him a wicked grin. "Not loud, huh?"

"Maybe a little loud during certain activities." He smiled down at me. "Stop distracting me with your sexy talk. I'm trying to be suave."

"Suave away."

"My point is, I looked up wrens, and I found some lore on them. You know, in some cultures, the killing of a wren is bad luck." He said, smoothing a strand of hair off my forehead. "Loss of cattle, broken bones, lightning strikes."

"That's some serious power a small bird can wield," I said.

"No more than they deserved." Cupping my cheek, he ran his thumb over my lower lip. "You have that power over me, you know."

The moment became too tense; we were barreling onto an unknown road, and I never made the right turn. Ducking my head down, my words were directed at his chest. "You can't say those sweet words to me if you don't mean them. I just got over someone, and I don't have the capacity for another heartbreak."

"I would never do anything that would hurt you." The sincerity in his voice chipped away at a little piece inside me. He had a great voice for empathy, tenderness, and full of understanding. I wished it could envelop me and stay with me forever.

My words were fragile as they came out, my gaze far away as if summoning the courage to say them. "You would never try. It doesn't mean this won't end painfully."

"I mean every word. I've never felt this way about a woman. Who I was before, who you were with. It has no place between us. This is about me and you. There is no before, only now."

I sucked in a breath, the words falling away. He saw me. No one else saw it. For years, I told myself that the life I built was enough. That having someone was enough. But to feel this, to know how close I was to losing myself...

The killing of a wren is bad luck.

Moving my head from where it was on his chest, I gazed up at him. A deep crevice opened inside me, and I wanted to believe in his words.

If I let him, this man could shatter me into pieces. He made me want things that I never allowed myself to dream of. It was a dangerous sensation, to stare into his honest blue-green eyes and know I was falling hard into the unknown.

They were beautiful words, only thinking of the present. But the future was fast approaching, and in a matter of twenty-four hours, I was destined for home. Not here with this gorgeous man who helped me down from his truck, made me crepes, and called me by a name no one else had. Not with this man I was growing to fall in love with.

Pulling away, I made a show of checking my phone. "I should head back to the cabin. I'm behind on a few reports, and strictly speaking, I'm not on vacation from work."

In Adrian's expression was a fight to argue, but he held his tongue. He helped me find my discarded clothes and walked me to the cabin. Despite my assurances that I was warm enough, he built me a fire in a matter of minutes so I wouldn't get cold. I refused his offer to make me a snack for later, giving him a quick but smoldering kiss and promising to return in a few hours once my reports were submitted. As he walked away, I watched his back. The long lines of him, with his hands in his pockets and his head down to protect his face from the icy wind. Hope bloomed in my chest. Maybe this was something I could hold on to. Maybe he could be mine.

Adrian

A s dawn broke, I woke to Wren beside me. Her face slack, her pink silk bonnet on her head, and her bare shoulder a warm bronze in the early morning light. A quick kiss to that soft area between her neck and her collarbone. With a tentative finger, I traced the line of her face, the shadows under her eyes, and the curve of her lip. This is what waking up every morning should be if only I had enough to be worthy of it.

With Wren back at the cabin, I busied myself with cleaning up the house. I thought about what I might make for dinner that night. How I would ask her to stay longer. The woodpile was getting low, so I grabbed a few more logs from the side porch to bring inside. Maizie took off, chasing a small animal and barking like a maniac. Her little tongue hanging out, she ran past me to the other cabin. Already, she had chosen her person, and I was no longer it. It didn't escape my notice the way she curled up beside Wren in bed and followed her around my home. Little traitor.

Whistling, I called her back to me. My arms heavy with wood, I heard the heavy footsteps on my porch. They didn't sound like the soft padding of Wren as she came over. How odd that I already knew the sound of her footsteps.

Dropping the wood by the stove, I stopped at the bottom to look at the shadow through my door. It was a man—I could tell that much. Frowning, I opened the door.

He stood a head shorter than me, skinny, with dirty-blond hair. Clad in a puffy jacket and snow pants, lift tickets for Vail, Alta, and Breckenridge still hanging from the hook on his hip.

"Can I help you?" I asked.

The guy blinked at me a few times, obviously surprised to see me. He rocked back on his heels and studied the numbers of my house. "Isn't this 143 Sitka?"

My arms crossed against my chest, I looked the guy up and down. He didn't look like someone peddling religion, and he sure as hell wasn't selling cookies. "It is."

"Uh, is there another 143 Sitka? 'Cause I put this in my GPS and ..." Maizie came up, jumping on him. Her little paws left small brown spots on his jacket. The man stepped back, swearing and brushing mud off his coat. "What the fuck, man? This is Moncler!"

"Who?" I asked, grabbing my dog before she got hurt.

The guy glared at me as he wiped the little footprints off his white coat. "I wouldn't expect someone like you to know what that is."

My patience had worn thin with this guy on my porch. Who insults another man's dog and him at his own home? "You still haven't told me who you are or why you're on my front porch."

"Beaufort Terrence Rebel Lark the Fourth." He stared me down as if the name should be impressive.

Scoffing, I shook my head. What a ridiculous name... Then it dawned on me. "You're Buck."

This guy was the ex? I couldn't be the best at determining what was attractive in a guy, but this boy was not what I expected.

He raised his chin. "How did you know that?"

Not owing him an explanation, I shoved my feet in the boots beside the door and pushed past him down the steps.

Wren opened the door, her amber eyes lighting as she saw me. A good sign. "Hey, I was just about to…" Her voice trailed off as she caught sight of Buck behind me.

"Oh." A darkness descended over her face as she took him in. Her eyes darted between me and Buck.

Buck brushed past me, walking to her side. "Wrenny, do you have any idea how long it took me to find this place? It's out here in butt-fuck nowhere. I don't know why you wanted to come here. It's not as bad as that place in Kevo's Pond we went to last summer, though. That was wild, right? Remember how the bathroom doorknob broke off in your hand and I had to get maintenance to let you out?"

Her face still, a frozen mask of uncertainty. He leaned in, kissing her on the cheek. The move so familiar between them, I could tell it was a reflex by now. She didn't push him away. Instead, she leaned into the kiss. That's what they had together. Reflexive touches inside jokes. Her eyes wide as they darted to me. In the short time I knew her, I had seen many expressions on her face: annoyance, sadness, glee. But I had never seen such heavy guilt clouding her features.

"So, you two met."

"Yeah, he showed me over here. The directions you had sucked, by the way." Buck turned to face me. "I didn't catch your name, though, man."

I waited for a moment, hoping that Wren would introduce us, that she would tell him who I was to her. That I could know what I was to her.

Say I'm yours.

"Buck, this is Adrian. He's, um. He's been, well. He…" With a shaky breath and fidgeting fingers, she gulped audibly.

"I'm the neighbor." Stepping to the side, I waved him up the stairs. I didn't hide the disappointment flooding through me at her hesitancy. "I'll leave you to each other."

Back in my house, I watched out the window as she let him in the front door. The easy smile he gave her and the way he was exactly the right height for her small stature. He didn't hulk over her. They complemented each other.

She never said what he did, but from the look of him, he had a good-paying job. He probably didn't have to buy value-brand cookies and do his own oil changes. Not that he looked like the kind of man who knew how to change his oil. But some women liked that. Wren had liked that, or she wouldn't have been with him for so long. And now, he was here to get her back. There could be no other reason for him to drive a hundred miles to this mountain town just to chat.

After about thirty minutes of watching the house and seeing nothing of interest, I shoved my feet back into my boots and headed to town. There was no way she was going to get back together with that guy, right?

Maybe?

Shaking my head as I walked into the grocery store, I decided I needed to get food for dinner, anyway. If Wren sent him away, we could talk and have a meal together. If not, well, I could eat leftovers for a few days.

Between the oranges and apples, I turned to the sound of my name being called.

Clark was standing by the glass case of donuts, a small bakery bag in his hand.

"Hey, man!" He did the bro handshake he gave to everyone. Normally, I liked seeing Clark. He was fun to be around for boarding and parties. But at nine a.m., when all I wanted to do was get back in the warm bed with Wren, he was the last person I wanted to get caught up with.

"Hey."

Hands stuffed in his pockets, he rocked back on his heels. "Tam told me about your little lady friend. Said she's real hot."

A rumbling heat was creeping up my neck at the description. I knew Tam wasn't the type to say something like that about Wren, but Penny would. Without thinking about the way Clark would take it, I could see Penny spilling all the details of our double date.

"Right," I said back, hoping he'd get the hint. "Um, her name is Wren. She's renting the cabin across from me."

"Nice, easy access, right? Got to love the conveyor belt of pussy we get around here, huh?" He laughed, a bawdy loud thing that made Mrs. Norris at the other end of the bagged salad display glance up in alarm.

I raised a hand to wave, my face growing warm, my eyes not looking at Clark. "It's not like that."

"What? This girl? Tam said she's from out of town. What else could it be?"

I wasn't in the mood to have a conversation about my burgeoning relationship with Clark of all people, in Icicle Creek Market of all places. "Something, I don't know."

"Whoa, are you actually into this chick?" he laughed at the comment. "No way. Is the player getting all pussy whipped?"

Frowning, I grabbed a lemon, tossing it in my cart. "I'm not pussy whipped."

"Of course not. How could you be? You're the man, after all. The guy who fucked two different chicks on the slopes on the same day."

I wanted to say that was a long time before I met Wren, but it was only a few months before the passing of my grandparents. "I'm not trying to be that guy anymore."

"Yeah, okay." He laughed. "I mean, it's not like you're really into this girl. You? We all know you're great for fun with the ladies, but you've always been the *bag 'em and tag 'em* type. Some of us aren't meant for commitment, and that's okay. I get it. I'm the same way. Know your strengths, man. Chaining ourselves to one vag? No, thank you. How does that even work? I don't know, and neither do you."

He laughed again, as if we were commiserating.

I studied this guy in front of me. The red-rimmed eyes. The broken blood vessels on his nose. Is this who I wanted to be? It was a lonely life being alone in that cabin with only my dog. As a new twenty-one-year-old, I would go to the bar and see those old men belly up at the bar, flirting with the bartender. The way they thought they had a chance with them, their faces bloated and veiny as the night wore on. Their too-loud laughs and chants of *Come on, sweetheart. A little smile wouldn't hurt*, between cruel jokes about their ex-wives.

Is that my future?

Deep down, I knew, while Clark's disgusting comments were a simplification, there was a shard of truth that was embedding itself in my mind. As much as I wanted Wren around, I didn't have the first idea of how to be in a relationship. What happened a week down the road, two? A year? All I had was the theoretical knowledge from other people. I didn't know how to actually be there for someone else. And Wren deserved someone who would treat her better. Someone who knew what he was doing.

I wasn't that man.

I gave a mumbled goodbye, grabbing the rest of my items in a daze. Back in the truck, I leaned my head against the steering wheel. Sitting in the same spot where Wren had ridden me only a day before. The same spot where she opened her eyes as she moved as the world tilted beneath me and all I knew was I wanted her to stay.

But now, in the light of morning, without her beside me, the insidious words crept in. My parents told me I didn't know how to take things seriously. Clark and his assumptions about what kind of man I was. The way women in the town would flirt casually. The careless way my previous flings would leave. Who was to say that Wren didn't feel the same? Yes, I was experiencing emotions I didn't know were possible to exist for another person. But she was leaving me, just like all the other women did. As much as I felt different, how could I know she did? She told me herself she was getting out of a long-term relationship, that I was a rebound was the likeliest scenario.

With Wren, I wanted to believe that falling for her would be enough. But it wasn't. I didn't need years of experience in relationships to know that a novice like me was bound to make mistakes.

My thoughts of the previous night of asking her to stay were flawed in the daylight. I couldn't ask her, not anymore. Not unless I was sure that was what she wanted.

Turning the truck on, I listened to the rumble of the engine before putting it in drive to make my ascent up to my mountain. Was I enough for someone like Wren? I had no experience in this, no way of knowing if I was going to get it right. A few blocks down from the grocery store, I stopped at a red light, three cars back from the intersection. My head hitting the headrest, I glanced to the right into Marta's diner. Framed like something out of a Hallmark movie was Wren sitting across from Buck. Even the window had the sprayed-on snow paint and little gold and red ornaments hanging across green garland. Transfixed, I watched as he reached across the table, taking her hand and lacing his fingers with hers. The same hand I held hours before. *Pull away, dammit. Push him off.* I willed her to leave him for daring to touch what was no longer his. But she didn't. She smiled at him, that beautiful bright smile. The smile that made me feel like I had swallowed the sun and would be warm forever. The smile I wanted to wake-up to every morning. A smile that never belonged to me. Behind me, a driver was leaning on their horn, the street before me empty. I gunned my engine, barely making my way across the intersection before the light turned red.

It might be nothing. They had been together for years, and there was bound to be something between them. She never promised me a thing. Maybe I had taken the high of finding her on my porch as a sign from my grandparents. Maybe this was all in my head. Turning onto the mountain road, doubt tickled at the back of my throat.

Wren

THERE WERE SO MANY things I wished I could have said to Adrian. Someone more skilled would have handled the situation with more grace and aplomb. Instead, I gaped at him like some wide mouth trout and could barely get the intelligible words together to make a sentence. Adrian probably thought I was a colossal idiot. *Again.*

There was a moment where I should have said something to Buck, but what was there to say on the front porch seconds after seeing the man you've been sleeping with and your ex-boyfriend standing there together?

It wasn't as if I was going to make some declarations while standing in my socks and oversized cardigan.

But maybe I should have.

Who knew what Adrian wanted from me? And now, I needed to get rid of Buck. Knowing my ex, he was oblivious to the tension between me and Adrian. An uneasiness crept into my stomach at the way Adrian stared at me before he walked away. Should I have chased him down, made sure he had nothing to worry about with Buck?

This was all new to me. Navigating these fraught situations was never a skill I possessed, thus my terrible introduction.

My sweater wrapped tighter around me. I studied Adrian's house. I couldn't tell where he was. Was he thinking about me? There was no way he thought I'd get back with Buck, right?

With a head shake, I let that thought go. Surely not. He had to know me enough by now. Resolute, I formed a plan. I would talk to Buck, make it clear that we were just friends and that whatever scheme he had for showing up here wasn't going to work. Knowing him, he was probably horny and figured I'd be lonely enough to get back together, if only for a few days.

I huffed out a low laugh at the idea. Sleeping with Buck would be borderline boring after being Adrian. That man had ruined me for all other men. Just the idea of Buck's skinny dick and weird, stabby thrusts made my lips turn up in disgust.

A low sound of the water being turned off sounded from down the hall, and I turned to find Buck emerging from the bathroom, a towel wrapped around his waist. "The water pressure here sucks."

Digging my nails into my forearms, I frowned at him. "Make yourself at home, why don't you?"

He laughed, as if my comment was the least bit funny. "Home, right. This place is such a dump. They don't even have cell reception out here. Why you insisted on this spot is beyond me."

A scratching heat simmered under my skin. "What do you want, Buck?"

Dropping his towel, he stood naked in the front room as he dug through his bag for his clothes. "I told you I couldn't get a hold of you and got worried."

"Did you stop to consider that maybe I didn't want to talk to you?"

"No, why wouldn't you?"

Under my finger, the scar behind my ear depressed. I rubbed it a few times, taking a gulp of air. I opened my mouth to speak, but Buck interrupted me before I could get the words out. "Let's go eat. My treat. We can talk there."

While I didn't see the point, I nodded my head. I didn't want to spend more time with Buck, but the idea of being only feet away from Adrian and not being with him was far worse. Once I sent Buck on his way, I could resume whatever this was between me and Adrian.

"Fine. Lunch. I'll drive."

We took my car. I didn't want Buck to have control over where we went and when we would leave. Even though it had been three days in this town, it was mine. Once in the car, he fiddled with my radio, connecting his phone to play his music.

"Can you not do that?" I asked as he pushed buttons on my console.

"I have to reconnect my phone. It's not showing up on here anymore."

"Gee, I wonder why," I quipped, rolling my eyes. Buck didn't seem to notice, still helping himself to my stereo. His White-boy rap on, he sat back in his seat, singing along to the song.

As always, I made two wrong turns while trying to find my way downtown. As we passed the bustling area of the riverside stores, I put my blinker on to turn into one of the paid parking lots.

"No, not here. These places are too busy. You know anywhere quieter?" he asked.

"I don't know. I haven't really had a chance to visit all the spots here."

"You've been here three days. What have you been eating?" His question went unanswered as he pointed at something across the street. "There, that place is empty. Let's go to that café."

I knew before looking it was Marta's place. "No, not there. You wouldn't like it. Greasy-spoon type place."

"I've been to a Denny's once. How bad could it be?"

A glance at his expensive snow jacket and three-hundred-dollar jeans told a different story. "Right, I don't want to hear complaining when we get in there."

Once we parked, Buck walked to the right of me on the sidewalk. I tried to slow my pace so we weren't beside each other, but he matched me. As we were about to the door, a car drove by, splashing muddy slush up over my legs and all over my newly cleaned jacket.

The sound I let out was halfway between a gasp and a scream. Buck smiled at me, holding his hand over his mouth, "Whoa, sorry, Wrenny. Glad that didn't get me."

With narrowed eyes, I stomped closer to the door, trying to shake the bulk of the gray slush off me. At the door, Buck stood behind me as I opened it, his eyes on his phone. An older man was beside the hostess sign, about to walk out. The door opened, and Buck walked in first, passing the man who had to stop on the other side.

Frowning, I blew out a deep huff through my nose, shaking my head. The older man's eyes darted from me to Buck, who was standing inside, his hand shoved in his pockets as he glanced around. I gave the older man a polite smile, waving him through the door before I walked in.

As he passed me, the man tipped his head. "Thank you, young lady. Always nice to see some courtesy." The second glance at an oblivious Buck wasn't lost on me.

"Have a good day, sir." The door slammed shut behind me as I stepped up to the hostess stand. Marta came out of the kitchen, her hair in that same tight bun at her nape, the apron she wore proclaiming *hot stuff coming through*. She saw me first, a bright smile stretching her face. "Wren, you came back."

"Hi, Marta."

Her eyes darted from me and darkened on Buck. She didn't have to say a word for me to know her thoughts.

I should've insisted we go anywhere but here. Marta was going to talk to Adrian about this for sure. I had no idea where we stood, but this wouldn't endear me to one of his oldest family friends.

Her tone noticeably icier, she jerked her head to the side. "Sit where you'd like. I'll bring out some water."

Buck headed to the other side of the room, pulling out the chair for the same table Adrian and I were at a few days before.

"Not there," I barked. My eyes darting around, I quickly grabbed a chair a few tables down. "Let's sit here. Closer to the window."

Shrugging, Buck sat down across from me. Marta came with our waters. Buck requested lime slices for him. Marta raised a brow at me with a look of disappointment. I hoped my repentant expression was enough.

"I got to take a leak," Buck announced, his chair scraping loudly in the restaurant.

He wasn't gone more than fifteen seconds before Marta came back to the table, dropping off a small bowl of lime slices, her arms crossed and a venomous grimace on her face.

"I don't appreciate you bringing your new boy toy into my restaurant. I may give Adrian a hard time, but that boy is like a grandson to me."

"It's not like that. Buck is my ex. I swear. Nothing is going on."

A condescending snort, and Marta rolled her eyes. "Is that so?"

"Yeah, I'm trying to tell him to leave. I don't want anything to do with him anymore. He's not who I want to be with, trust me."

Her gaze softened, from vicious to skeptical. "You better not break my boy's heart, you hear?"

With a sigh of relief, I saw Buck emerge from the bathroom. "I don't plan on it."

We ordered. I got the same burger I had last time, and Buck had a steak salad. Well done. Marta left us, giving me a pointed glare that let me know I had one chance and not to squander it.

"So, you want to tell me why you're here?" I asked.

"I wanted to see you," he said plainly, taking a sip of his water and grimacing. "This water is gross. I'm getting a soda." He raised his hand to snap at Marta, and I grabbed it, slamming it against the table.

"Don't do that. It's rude."

"It's their job." He snorted out a low laugh. "When did you get all bleeding heart?"

"I've always found it rude when you did that. Only now that we're no longer together I can tell you and don't have to worry about you sulking about it."

"I don't sulk." He scoffed, affronted.

Rolling my eyes, I focused on the subject at hand. Mainly on how to get whatever this was out of the way so I could send him back to whatever he was doing. "Whatever, it doesn't matter. How did you find me, Buck?"

"You emailed me the itinerary, remember? When you made the reservation?"

"You mean the email where you told me you'd put your credit card down to pay for it since it was a late birthday present?" I asked, exasperation clinging to my words.

He had the good sense to appear chagrined. "After we broke up, I figured you'd cancel the trip. Take care of it, like you always do."

It didn't hurt this time to hear those words. The woman who did all those things for him was a different person than the one I am today. "Like I did. Past tense. Like our relationship, which is over."

He reached to take my hand, lacing his fingers between mine. "Don't be like that, Wrenny."

Frozen at his audacity, I stared at our hands entwined. For years, I craved this touch, the softness of his palm against mine and the loving expression in his eyes. Now it felt flat. There was no buzz of electricity, no pulse of need. It was skin-to-skin, a warm hand against warm hand and nothing else.

"Look, I don't know why you decided this was the right time to chase me down. Maybe you were bored—maybe you were horny and figured I'd be an easier lay than the effort to pick up some random girl at the bar. But I'm not interested."

"Maybe I want you back. Did you think of that? We had a good thing. I love you." His words sounded sincere, but I knew the tone, the way his eyes would grow soft as much as I knew how to tie my shoes. It was all so familiar, and it was all so hollow.

I smiled big at him. The change in power dynamics was hilarious to me. For years, I chased this man's approval, tying his affection into my self-worth. "No, you don't. I'm not sure if you ever loved me. What I know is you loved what I did for you. You loved how I made you feel about yourself. But honestly, it was never love because, if you had truly known me, you would have seen how miserable I was for years."

"You weren't miserable. We had some great times together. What about last summer, when we went parasailing? Or when we made love on the beach of Playa del Carmen."

"I remember all that differently. You went parasailing, I threw up over the side of the boat for an hour. And as for the sex on the beach, I was recovering from the sand burn for weeks after that." Pulling my hand away, I scraped my hand over my face. "And I won't argue with you about it."

"So, that's it. You're just going to give up on three years together like it was nothing?"

"I didn't give up on us, Buck. You were the one who ended it." My voice was soft.

"I made a mistake. I'm here to tell you I want you back."

Could this man take a hint? I wasn't this needy when he dumped me months before. I accepted it, then cried in my shower to "Sad Beautiful Tragic" the way my lord and savior, Taylor Swift, decreed it.

"I can't go back. It wasn't a mistake for me. All that between us needs to stay in the past. I don't regret being with you. But I don't want to be with you anymore."

"I get it. You're still mad at me. What do I need to do? Flowers, candy. I'll take you to that art show in Seattle you've been bugging me about. What will it take?"

All these words, I would have loved a few months ago. Now, they fell like stones. "Nothing, Buck. I don't want a single thing from you. You're a good guy, sometimes, and I'm sure somewhere out there is a girl that you will make happy. But that's not me."

He leaned forward, his face serious. "Look, I was going to wait until we had a fancy dinner tonight or something, but I got you something to make up for all this."

I couldn't imagine what he thought would make up for years of a terrible relationship. His cell out, he slid it over to me. The screen showing an email from an expensive cruise line.

"You booked a cruise?"

His face broke into a huge grin. "Yeah, all expenses paid, excursions, drinks, whatever you want."

I fought back the hysterical bubble rising in my chest. How many times did this man see me green with sickness on a lake? He thought I would want to be in the middle of the ocean? "That's not going to work. I'm not going on a cruise with you, Buck."

"What? Why?"

"Because I don't want to be with you." There were so many reasons, but really, didn't it boil down to this in the end?

He scoffed. "Do you think you're going to find a better guy than me? I'm the best you'll ever get."

Sighing heavily, I leaned back in my chair. I didn't have the fight in me. There was nothing of worth between us any longer. "We both know that's not true."

"Oh yeah, who's going to have you now?" He laughed for a moment before the smile fell from his face. "Wait, did you sleep with that guy? What's his name, Archie?"

"His name is Adrian, and I'm not answering that question."

"Why, because you did? You're unbelievable. I can't believe you would do that to me." His words got louder. "That's who you want to be with, some poor, scruffy guy who lives in the woods of fucking nowhere? Over me?"

"Believe it or not, who I date has nothing to do with you. That man is five times the man you are. I've only spent three days with him, and it was better than all three of our *years* together."

"You barely know the guy. He's just using you. Guys like that, they see a girl like you and know you're only good for one thing."

Pushing off, I stood up, grabbing my purse. "I don't have to listen to this. The moment we broke up, I stopped owing you a thing."

"Wait, where are you going? You drove me here. My car is still at the cabin."

"I told you I'm not doing a single thing for you anymore. Take a cab. You've got the money, since you're so rich and all."

Stalking toward the front of the diner, I handed Marta a ball of cash to pay. I wasn't sure if I was short or not, but she waved my money away.

"Don't you worry about paying. You go get that boy."

"What about Buck?" I asked her.

She glanced over my shoulder at him, still sitting at the table, his face red. "He better pay, or I'll have the police pick him up."

The cold winter air was welcome on my heated cheeks, a sense of right-eousness flowing over me. I'm sure the town would be talking about the exchange for weeks, but I didn't care. Buck had made his own nine-hun-dred-thread count sheet bed, and now he could lay in it.

Driving back up the mountain road, a sense of calm set over me. For the first time in my life, every turn I took was the right one. After a lifetime of never being sure where I was headed, I knew this path was true.

Not bothering to go back into the rented cabin, I parked beside Adrian's truck and made my way up his porch. The snow crunched under my boots as I walked the small pathway. I'd have to get my things from the cabin later, but now that I had officially said my piece with Buck, I didn't want to waste any more time in that other cabin. Knocking a few times, I listened as Maizie's little nails tapped on the wood floor alongside Adrian's footsteps. The door swung open, and Adrian was there, the warmth of his house radiating through the doorway. Early afternoon light shone over him, highlighting the gold in his scruff, the line of his jaw.

"Hey," I breathed out, a smile widening my face. He glanced down at me, his eyes catching on my hands clasped in front of me. A slow sense of dread crept up my body as his face remained stony.

"Where's your boyfriend?" he asked, his knuckles white on the door frame.

"Um, not here. And he's not my boyfriend," I corrected.

"Could have fooled me."

A shiver ran down my body, from the cold of the air and from the ice in his tone. "Can I come in? It's chilly out here."

"It's not a good time. I was about to head out to see Tam and Penny."

"Could I come—I mean, do you want me to come with you and see…"

His eyes kept darting away, his hands shoved in his pockets as he bounced on the balls of his feet. My words trailed off. I was getting the hint.

"No. I think it's best if you stay here." His eyes set on Buck's car still parked in front of the other cabin.

"Did something happen? Did I say something? I know I should have introduced you and Buck better, but I was caught off guard, and to be honest, with him, less is more. I figured it wasn't worth the long, drawn-out conversation."

Granted, it was one I had later with Buck, but I wanted to spare Adrian. There was no need for him to be caught in the middle of it.

A muscle ticked in his jaw as he stared down at me. "It's fine. It's whatever, right? Just like us. We had fun, but you're leaving tomorrow morning, anyway. You weren't going to stay."

I hugged myself tighter, a chill that had nothing to do with the cold seeping into my bones. "Could I come in and we could talk about it?"

"What's there to talk about, *Wrenny*?"

I hated the nickname on his lips, hated the way it curled and spoiled in his mouth. He spit it like an expletive.

Beyond hope, I tried to make my voice as even as possible, trying not to betray the churn of sadness boiling up inside me. "You know, I thought what we had between us was special, that these days together were happy."

"I'm not here to make you happy," he snapped. "And I don't need you to make me happy."

The words were like a slap. I reared back with the force of them.

I don't need you.

Don't need you.

"Oh. Of course." Buck's words from earlier echoed in my head. How could my asshole ex see something that I couldn't? He was right. Adrian didn't really want me. I was just another tourist fling, like the rest of them. Wrapping my arms right against my chest, I willed myself to keep the tears at bay until I could turn and walk away. "Right. You're right. We barely know each other. Sorry if I was too much."

With the ball of my foot, I turned away, stalking down the now well-known path between the houses. I could hear Adrian calling out for me to hold on, to wait, to let him explain. But I wasn't going to stand there and listen to whatever chivalrous explanation he was trying to make. He might have wanted to soften the blow of his words now, but the message was clear.

Over my shoulder, I shouted, "This Wren hopes you lose all your cattle and get hit by lightning!"

I could hear the footsteps behind me, but I kept walking, stomping through the front door of the cabin and closing the door behind me. As I locked the deadbolt, I stared through the window to see Adrian standing at the halfway point between the cabins. His hands pushed into the pockets of his coat and a pained expression on his face.

Good, I hoped it hurt to reject me.

A low, vindictive space opened inside me. As I set the alarm, my eyes trained on him. After a minute, he shook his head at me, turning on his heels and retreating into his warm home.

Adrian

THE HORSE AND TRAILS was empty as I walked in. The TV was on in the corner, warning of a snowstorm that was forecast for the next few hours. Behind the bar, Jordan was wiping her phone, texting someone. Jordan put a finger up to tell me to wait as I settled onto the stool at the bar. A few seats down, someone left a half-empty glass of brown liquor with a coaster on top.

"Sorry, I was texting the wife to let her know I'll be closing up early at ten and to pick up batteries."

"Tell Janey I said hi."

She slid the phone back into her back pocket. "Will do. Now, what'll it be?" she asked.

What I wanted was the winter ale I had with Wren the first time we came here together, but I couldn't imagine drinking that now. "Double bourbon. Straight up."

She raised a brow but didn't argue, pouring my drink and setting it down in front of me. The whiskey burned my throat as I downed the whole thing. Setting the glass back down, I motioned for her to refill the glass, and Jordan complied, her frown deepening. "That's your last shot. I'm already dealing with one drunk asshole today. I don't need two."

Slamming the second shot down, I wiped my mouth. The fiery burn hurt as it warmed my chest. I welcomed the sensation, hoping it could numb the ache that was expanding inside my chest.

It was a mistake to come here. The moment I said those words, I wanted to take them back. Even if Wren was getting back together with Buck, even if I was some weekend-long fun, she didn't deserve to be talked to that way. She was obviously trying to be kind in telling me she was back together with her ex. Always kind, always the warmth I craved.

No, I made the right choice. I saw them together. I saw the way he looked at her, the way she leaned into his embrace, the fit of her hand in his. Wren and I had a weekend together. They had years. I would never be able to compete with that. It would be foolish to try.

Jordan set a light beer down in front of me beside a glass of water. My fingers warm, my head getting fuzzy. Ordinarily, I wasn't such a lightweight, but the four shots of whiskey were now taking effect.

To my left, a stool scraped loudly over the concrete floor as someone sat down at the bar. A quick glance had my pint of beer stopped halfway to my mouth. Wren's possible ex was sitting two spots down from me, his hand gripping around a tumbler of brown liquid stopped mid-air as he stared at me. We were mirror images of each other, frozen.

"What are you doing here?" he asked, his words slurred. So, this was the drunk asshole Jordan mentioned.

"Same thing as you, Bucko," I said, taking a large swig of my beer.

"It's not bad enough that you have to steal my girl, but now you've come here to gloat?" He downed the rest of his whiskey and frowned into the empty glass. "I get left at some crap diner, miles from my car, all my calls go straight to voicemail, and there's no taxis in the area until tomorrow, so

I have to get a hotel room. And now, right when I have a good buzz on, the asshole who's been fucking my girl comes and sits beside me."

I filed all that information away. Wren had left him in town. I didn't know the reasons, but it was sure to be a good one. The entire exchange I had with her at the cabin changed in my head. Maybe she wasn't trying to let me down but tell me she was done with Buck. And I pushed her away, like an asshole. Worse than this drunk guy beside me.

"Three years, we were together. I ask for a little time apart, and what does she do? Run off to this shithole town and find some redneck to fuck her."

On the other side of the bar, Jordan removed his empty glass and crossed her arm over her chest. "Knock it off, or you're out of here."

He waved his hand in a shooing motion. "Yeah, yeah. I'll behave. Sorry."

Jordan's eyes now lit on me. "You too, Adrian. Don't make me eighty-six you for the night."

"Loud and clear, Jo." My hands came up in surrender. Jordan narrowed her eyes at me and shook her head to let me know she meant business. Before she turned back to the bar to help another patron at the end, she put up two fingers, motioning between me and herself with the universal *I'm watching you* signal. I nodded back.

"You can't blame me for Wren's decisions."

He snorted, shaking his head. "Why shouldn't I? We were fine. Still texting all the time before she took this trip and then she got up here. All my calls go to voicemail. She isn't responding to the TikTok videos I send her. I drive the three hours it takes because, obviously, she's punishing me or something, and what do I find? You. According to her, you're five times the man I am. We were fine before she came here. You think you can swoop in with your ten-inch cock and magic tongue and take my place?"

I had to hold back a laugh at the description. Is that how Wren described me? Somehow, I doubted it, but I wasn't going to tell him to stop shouting it.

"I was going to surprise her with a vacation, a ten-night cruise in the Caribbean. All-you-can-eat-and-drink package, pool, water slides, the whole thing."

"Wren gets seasick," I reminded him, a crease furrowing my brow. Did he not know that? He had to, right?

Buck waved a hand at the comment as if to bat it away. "She would have been fine."

I snorted at his comment. *What kind of man buys a vacation that only one person would actually enjoy?*

"It's not funny. I love her." He slammed the empty glass down on the bar top. Jordan shouted for him to knock it off, hurrying over, but the die had been cast. This was edging into dangerous territory.

"Then, why did you dump her in the first place?" I was taunting him now. I wasn't sure if Wren truly wanted me, but at least she did not want to be with this guy anymore. To leave someone miles away from their car in an impending snowstorm was a brutal move.

"You sure know a whole lot about me." He stood up and walked toward me, trying to tower over me, but he was at least six inches shorter.

I leaned closer. "And why do you think that is? You'd be amazed at what a person hears during pillow talk. Can you picture it Wren in my bed, the things she said to me? The things I did to her..."

I should have seen the punch coming. I was goading him enough that it was a foregone conclusion to the night. On a normal night, I would have been able to dodge the hit, but after several drinks, my reflexes were dulled enough that his fist struck my cheek. Pain exploded in my eye as I stumbled back. Using the bar top as support, I stumbled back, barely able to stay on my feet from the blow. I'd give him this. He was a little bitch, but his swing was mighty.

Unfortunately, for him, he wasn't getting a second one. I took him down, tackling him to the floor, where I grabbed the front of his shirt and slammed his head into the floor. I landed one punch on his chin, and I heard the crack of his head hit the ground. Through my one good eye, I see the blood on his lip. Behind me, Jordan was yelling for both of us to get out of her bar. Buck laced an arm around my neck and pulled me down into a headlock. We rolled around on the floor, clumsy punches and stools falling down. At one point, my head hit a corner of a wall. My elbow hit his eye, it swelling up immediately into what would be a nasty black eye. After a minute of tussling, I got the upper hand, pulling my fist back to punch him when someone wrapped a forearm around my middle, pulling me up. I fought for a moment before a familiar voice in my ear told me to stop fighting.

I turned my head to see Tam holding me back.

"What the fuck, man?" I shouted as Buck was crab-crawling back until he could pull himself up and away from me.

"Knock it off. He's not worth it."

From a few feet away, Buck was wiping the blood off his lip, his face screwed up in anger. "Fuck you, man. You'll be hearing from my lawyer."

"For what?" Jordan asked. "I saw the whole thing. You threw the first punch. He was defending himself."

Buck's eyes darted around the bar at the few patrons who were watching. They all nodded at him, agreeing with Jordan. Snagging his coat off the ground, he pushed past me and Tam, who still had me locked in place.

At the door, he turned to glare back at me. "Fuck you, and fuck this town. I hope the lousy pussy's worth it."

I struggled against Tam again, this time wanting to blacken the other eye. Tam held tight. "He's not worth it."

The door slammed shut, and the bar was quiet. Once he was gone, the fight left me.

"Thanks, Jordan." I collapsed on the stool and buried my head in my hands.

"Don't thank me. You're the one who's paying for everything you broke, dumbass."

A small price to pay for knowing the town had my back. "Add it to my tab."

"Already done." She poured a beer for Tam and refilled my water glass. When I opened my mouth to ask for another beer, she shook her head and handed me a sandwich bag of ice. "Don't even think about it."

As the ice pack hit my cheek, I winced at the pain but held it there. "Where did you come from?" I asked Tam.

He took a long sip of his beer before setting it back on the coaster and rotating it until the decal faced him. "Jordan called me when you ordered your second shot. She said she had a bad feeling and that it would be a good idea for me to come get you."

Pulling the ice pack off my cheek, I set it on the bar top. "Thanks for having my back."

He snorted. "Come on, man. Of course, I would. Besides, Wren would never forgive you if you got sued by that pretty-boy douchebag."

Jordan walked by again, snapping her fingers and pointing at the ice pack, which I dutifully put back on my cheek.

"Not sure if Wren is going to forgive me in general. I fucked up with her." Grimacing, I rested my hand on the ice pack, pressing it into my cheek. The surface pain was subsiding into numbness, but my head was pounding.

Frowning at my statement, Tam handed Jordan his credit card to close out the tab. Grabbing his coat and mine, he ushered me out into the night. A few steps into my walk to my car, and he stopped me. "Where do you think you're going?"

"Sleep it off in my car."

Shaking his head, he pointed at his own truck. "Nope, Penny would never forgive me. Get in. You can crash on our couch."

After the adrenaline had wasted from my body, my muscles were screaming at me. Hobbling from Tam's truck to his living room, I ignored Penny's exclamations as I collapsed on their couch, kicking my shoes off and rolling to my side. The floral print velvet couch cocooned me. I sank into the upholstery and tried to fight the headache that was raging at the edge of my brain.

"I brought you a sleeping bag." Tam held up a large white bag in the air above me.

I waved my hand, and he dropped it on top of me. Fumbling around with the bag, I tried to find the zipper to climb in when Penny walked into the living room, her eyes on the bag.

"What are you doing with my wedding dress?"

"It's a sleeping bag," Tam corrected her.

Frowning, Penny stalked over to me, ripping the bag out of my hand and unzipping the front to show us the frothy white monstrosity inside the garment bag. "It's a wedding dress. This is its garment bag. Not for sleeping in or on." Her eyes narrowed on me.

My head was throbbing too much to process that I tried to sleep on top of a wedding dress. I lay back down on the couch. My eyes closed, I heard the hushed whispers of Tam and Penny in the kitchen. I caught words like, "fight," "fuckwit," and "a man's got to stick up for himself." Pain was radiating from my shoulder, up my neck, and back down the other side. As I shifted, the scrapes I had on my legs rubbed painfully against my jeans. I blew out a deep breath and counted down from one hundred until my mind grew blank and then there was darkness.

Minutes or hours later, it was hard to say which. The light was different on my aching eyes. The approaching footsteps had me opening one eye to find Penny standing over me with an ice pack in one hand and a murderous gaze in her eyes. "Hey, princess, glad to see you join us."

"What time is it?"

"Eight-thirty. Because of you, I had to stop watching my *Witch Academy* show. You owe me. I was about to find out whether Breslin could defeat the Infernal Obscuria and save the town."

Between the nonsense words and her sharp tone, my head pounded a battle against my skull. "I don't know what any of that means."

She settled in a chair across from me, surveying me with a narrowed gaze. "Does it hurt?"

"I've had worse."

She tossed the ice pack down beside me. "You're such a liar. You look like chopped prosciutto."

With a groan, I sat up, grabbed the ice pack, and pressed it to my throbbing cheek. "Way to make a guy feel better."

"Sounds like you deserved it."

"You should see the other guy."

Penny rolled her eyes, sitting back in her chair. "What happened?"

"Wren's ex and I had some words at the bar. I took offense to some things he said."

"Only him. You didn't do a thing?"

Dropping the ice pack, I looked across the pink-and-green decorated room at her. "I might have made a few colorful remarks."

"Why were you even at the bar? Shouldn't you be at home with Wren, confessing your undying love?"

That was what I should have been doing. Instead, I was here on this rose-patterned velvet couch, miles away from Wren.

"Can I say what happened and not have you two be assholes about it?"
I asked them. Tam nodded right away, but Penny narrowed her eyes.

"Depends on what happened."

"Of course we can." Tam insisted.

A warning glance passed between them, and Penny sighed. "Fine. I'll
refrain."

So, I told them as best I could about how I wanted to ask Wren to stay.
How her ex showed up, how I watched them together, how I ran into Clark
and wondered if he was right about me. Driving by them in the diner to see
them holding hands. The words I wanted to take back the moment they
were said. And worst of all, the pain in her eyes as she locked the door and
stared me down, daring me to come closer.

The way I, instead, ran away, drank myself stupid, and punched her ex.

"Wow, you fucked that one up." The words were no more than I expected, but they still stung.

Tossing the now lukewarm ice pack to the side, I glared at Penny. "What
happened to you not being an asshole?"

She snorted. "If you think I'm an asshole now, wait until I get going. I'm
about to be the biggest bitch you've ever seen. I can't believe you would
listen to Clark of all people. Not just listen to him but use that as some sort
of justification for not being with Wren."

Tam placed a hand on his wife's knee, soothing her. "Come on, Pen.
He's obviously in a bad spot. We don't need to make him feel worse."

"He should." She batted his hand away, sending him a death glare before
her eyes settled on me. "This is the first time you let yourself be open to
more than a casual fling, and you do exactly what you always do when you
come up against a wall. You take the easy way out. Instead of fighting for
her, asking her to stay, you say all the wrong things."

"She wasn't going to stay with me." If she wanted to before, she certainly
wasn't going to now.

"How do you know? Did you ask her? Or did you tuck tail and run off at the slightest bit of friction? Did you stay and hear her out? No, you listened to a guy who calls all women "vag holes." Which is not only terrible English but the most misogynistic thing ever. That guy is who you're taking relationship advice from?"

"Maybe he had a point? Why else would Wren be holding some other man's hand?"

Penny sat back, her eyes narrowing at me. "I don't know. You should have asked her. I know the concept of long-term relationships is novel to you, but breakups are messy. She was with the guy for three years. Do you really think she should send him away minutes after he shows up?"

"Yes," I said.

Her hand wiped over her face, she shot Tam an expression of *help me out here.*

"I wanted to ask her to stay with me," I repeated.

"And how was she supposed to know that? Did you tell her?"

I shook my head. "No, fucked up." The fight left me, and I buried my head in my hands. "I know I did. But what can I do now?"

Reaching out, Penny took my hand, pulling it from my face. "You talk to her. You don't jump to conclusions. And you tell her how you feel."

The break in my voice hurt as I spoke. "And if she doesn't want to stay with me?"

Penny shrugged. "Falling for someone is exactly that. Falling. Sometimes, we don't know where we'll land. But you're not going to know until you try. I know it's scary. Most worthwhile things aren't easy."

"That's the thing." I stared down at my hands. "It was easy. How I felt with her. It was exactly how my Gramps said it was with Gran. Simple and life-changing. Everything with her was effortless."

Wren standing on my porch, the light filtering through the little stray hairs loose from her braids. Wren's grin as she held that bag of cookies in the grocery store. The delicate touch of her finger against my jaw as she leaned in to kiss me. The spark in her eye when I helped her down from the truck. She had taken root in me, flowing through all the cracks and holes I had inside, sealing me together and changing everything.

"I need to talk to her." I jumped up, stumbling for my shoes. Tam stood up with me, concern ceasing his brow.

"How are you going to get there? You can't drive right now. Look outside."

A glance outside saw the snow piling up, fat white fluff blanketing the cars in the driveway. "I need to see her."

"It's a blizzard out there. Your truck is miles away, and even if I could get you to your truck, there's no way you could make it up that hill to your place," Tam argued.

"If you won't take me to my truck, I'll walk. But I'm going back home to her. One way or another."

Penny frowned, shaking her head. "It's at least three miles to the bar, Adrian."

Snagging my coat off the floor, I shoved my feet in my boots. "I don't care."

"Do you want breakfast before you try to hike in a blizzard?" Penny stood, taking two steps to the kitchen.

The memory of the overly salted bone-dry chicken and rice dish she shoved in my hands a month before made my stomach roll.

"No, I'm good." A glance at Tam had him raising his brows in agreement. "I'm going, one way or another."

From the corner of my eye, I watched as Penny and Tam did that weird couple telekinesis thing, having an entire conversation with brow raises and head tilts.

After a minute of their nonverbal exchange, Tam sighed loudly. "Fine! I'll drive you to your truck. But if you get stuck in the snow going up that hill, I'm not towing you out until the storm is over."

I nodded at him. I was ready to walk. Every inch closer to Wren was an inch I'd take.

Wren

F ROM MY SPOT AT the window, I watched as he got back in his truck. Waited for him to come back. Once the anger subsided, I was left with a dull ache that bloomed across my chest, burrowing deep.

When I was fourteen, I was dumped for the first time. Shane sat in front of me in English class and would twist in his seat to talk to the people around him. He had a big laugh and a pinky he broke when he was seven that was far shorter than the rest of his fingers. We were paired up to discuss *Lord of the Flies* together. He had thick, curly black hair he gelled to the point of it being rock hard and soft brown eyes. Our first kiss was outside his parent's house after trick or treating in his much more expensive neighborhood. He pulled up his Ghostface mask, and I leaned in on red sequined shoes, careful not to let the fake blood of his plastic knife get on my Dorothy Gale pinafore.

Three months later, my parents had moved us to Wellton, Arizona, and I was floundering at my new school. The phone call wasn't a surprise. It had been over a week since he returned my calls, and I heard from my one friend that Shane was talking to Lauren Blankenship in the hallway. Still, I cried that night. I cursed my parents for having us move yet again, cursing

Lauren Blankenship for being there when I wasn't and cursing Shane for not wanting me.

Reflecting on that moment, it all felt so silly and juvenile, but the aching that formed under my ribs, the crush in my lungs, and the tingle in my fingers was a wholly new experience. Over the years, I would be dumped again and would be the dumper. I would experience a shade of that pain again. But never again would the hurt be as fierce as the first time, clinging to the phone and begging him to reconsider.

Until today.

With Shane, with Buck. I thought I knew heartbreak, but nothing compared to the visceral pain of hearing those words from Adrian. My body splintered into a million pieces, all slicing edges on one another. I was shards. Somehow, I was able to get behind the door before breaking down.

As much as I told myself that how I felt for Adrian wasn't love, I knew it was wrong. Nothing else could hurt this much. I wasn't only losing Adrian. It was the life I had built in my mind, the home I created in this town, and the life I finally wanted to call my own.

So many wrong turns in my life to lead to his front steps. While I could kid myself that it wasn't serious, I wasn't going to lie to myself.

Loving Adrian was never wrong, but maybe he could be my path to something new. Even if he was no longer on the road with me.

Adrian didn't come back, and neither did Buck. Briefly, I wondered what happened to him. He would have to get his car at some point, but I wouldn't make it easy for him. Knowing him, he got a hotel room downtown and was currently drinking his sorrows away with some local lady. That the image of Buck taking some woman back to his hotel room didn't bother me at all proved I had made the right call. I should have done it months before.

Hours passed, and eventually, I wandered from the window where Adrian wouldn't be and to the kitchen. There were a few cans of wine left over from my shopping trip. I was leaving in the morning, alone, and, if I was persistent, hungover. I started on the white wine, the cold sharp taste welcome on my tongue. On a plate, I piled cheese and meat, almonds and satsuma pieces. My own charcuterie plate. Between gulps of canned wine, I shoved the food into my mouth, tall stacks of crackers, cheese, and salami. Pulp from the small oranges stuck to my fingers and gathered dust from the nuts. It wasn't graceful; it was gluttony. But no one was around to see my feast.

The first can drained, and I opened the second. My plate empty, I glanced out the window at Adrian's dark house. Where was he? Meeting a new tourist in town? Seeing that beautiful blonde, Layla? It was so easy to fall under his spell, to think that maybe I could be more for him. But he obviously didn't want that. Once again, I was foolish for a man.

Clutching the can to my chest, I watched the snowflakes as they came down, lush white bits floating in the darkened air. The front of my car was already obscured by the thin layer accumulating. How I was getting out tomorrow, I wasn't sure, but that was a tomorrow issue. Tonight was for canned wine and wallowing.

Pulling my sweater closer around me, I shivered in the chilling cabin. Adrian had built me a fire when I was working earlier, but the logs burned down hours before. Eyeing the stack of kindling and logs beside the stove, I wrinkled up my nose. What was the first step again?

It was all easier when Adrian was here to show me. Another big glug of wine down the hatch, and I gathered what seemed like enough sticks and various stuff to start a fire. The process took me over thirty minutes, two burned fingertips, countless pieces of wood, and over ten sheets of newspaper before the fire grew enough to catch the kindling on fire.

Content with my good work, I slapped my hands together and glanced around the cabin to gloat. No one is here to see my accomplishment. Another glance out the window, and still, Adrian's truck is not back. It's dark now, an inky-blue vastness outside. Dark and cold. Taking a sip of my wine, I narrowed my eyes at the empty house. He left for who knows how long. Left me and, more importantly, left his dog. That poor puppy.

Well, that won't do. Before I could think about the millions of reasons, it was a terrible idea I was stalking to the door. I shoved my feet into my boot and pulled my coat on. Beneath my feet, the new powder sank down as I trudged across the way. Fat, cold flakes clung to my hair and shoulders as I made my way onto his front porch. Testing the knob, I was unsurprised to find it unlocked. A quick stomp of my feet to clean off the snow, and I was inside. Maizie came down the stairs at my entrance.

"Don't worry, girl. I'm here to rescue you. You can have salami and gouda with me. We'll have a girl's night." Maizie blinked at me with her big brown eyes, her big tongue lolling out of her mouth. I scoop her up, stuffing her inside my coat, which I zipped up until her head stuck out the top, and we made our way back across the street. Halfway over, I let her down so she could do her business before coming back inside.

Now, with the two of us in the cabin, I made her a doggy plate, setting it on the floor beside a bowl of water. Maizie ate all the food and then jumped up on the couch with me, where I was still nursing my second can of wine.

I ran my fingers through her thick, wiry fur as she closed her eyes. What will Adrian think when he shows up back at his house and finds his dog missing? Dognapped.

It was an odd reversal of the woman who took all his silverware but left Maizie. I wasn't going to keep her, even if I was upset with the way he treated me. I wasn't a monster. It was dog sitting. Without permission.

What a mess I was.

Draining the second can, I went to set it on the floor beside the couch, and it slipped from my fingers, rolling away. Laying on my side, I glared at the errant can where it rested under the coffee table. One eye shut, I reached out for the can as far as my arm can go. My fingers brushed the can, but it rolled further away, the slippery thing. Again, I reached out, my nails brushing the can before my body tilts and I'm falling off the couch and onto the floor. Maizie jumped down, licking my forehead and nudging me.

"I'm getting up," I slurred, pulling myself up onto my hands and knees. From the new angle, I was able to reach under the table and grab the wayward can. With one eye to focus, I read the back of it. Oh, geez. That explains it.

"Did you know there are three glasses of wine in one of these?" I asked the dog, showing her the can and holding up three fingers. She cocked her head to the side and stared at me. "Yeah, me nee-fer."

The can clunked loudly on the coffee table. I used both hands to pull myself up and onto the couch. Sinking into the soft fabric, I fell to the side, lying down. Once again, Maizie lay beside me, curling up at my stomach. "I'll get up in a minute, and we'll go to bed, okay, Maizie Girl?"

The soft heat of her furry body and the heaviness of my eyelids were the last thing I remembered as I drifted off.

The light was wrong, too bright on my face when the morning sun shouldn't be able to shine directly through the window to my right. Dragging my face across the rough fabric, my eyes squeezed shut. Stale and gritty, I ran my dry tongue over my teeth. Two cans of wine were the worst idea I ever had. With one eye open, I saw Maizie curled up beside me on the couch. Right, because I didn't make it up the stairs to the bed. Okay, two cans of wine, dognapping, and sleeping on a cheap futon were the worst ideas I ever had.

As I stumbled to my feet and into the bathroom, Maizie followed behind me, her little nails tapping on the wood floor. I made quick work of scrubbing my face and brushing my teeth if only to get last night's mistakes from soaking in worse.

My hair was a knotty mess that took far too long to untangle enough to be semi-presentable. My aunties used to tell me I was too tender-headed, but it hadn't hurt to comb my hair out in years. Until today. I felt like I was seven sitting at the table while my Aunt Dee raked and pulled at my scalp to get my curls to cooperate. Everything hurt, from my toenails to my eyebrows. Retreating to the couch, I collapsed on my butt, slapping a warm washcloth over my face and breathing in deeply. Boom, boom, boom. My brain battered against my skull, and I cursed the second can of wine, cursed Buck for this trip, and cursed my own foolish mind for thinking that what I felt for Adrian could have been real.

Summer had been right. When was I ever attracted to a nice guy? My picker was definitely broken if I thought I could be different for a guy like Adrian. I knew what he was. It was obvious by the way he got his dog, the surprise in his friends when I was brought around. Obvious to everyone but me, we'd never be more than a fling. Once again, I was silly enough to think that I could be an exception when all I would ever be was the rule.

A low rumble of an engine from far away sounded, and I pulled the wet washcloth off my face to angle my face to the window. Creeping down Sitka Lane was Adrian's white truck. Chunks of snow piled on the hood slid off as he parked the truck in front of his house. Ducking down beneath the window, I sat on my knees to peek out across the street. I watched as Adrian walked up his steps, hand on the knob, before shaking his head and glancing back at my cabin.

"Crap." I ducked down low, hoping he didn't catch me watching him. Lying flat on my back, I held my breath as if that would help the situation.

Counting by threes, I tried to calm my erratic heartbeats. Instead, they grew louder, steadier.

Nope, that wasn't my heart beating loud in my ears. That was Adrian's footsteps as he climbed the porch and knocked on the front door.

From the other end of the couch, Maizie gazed at me with an expression saying, *Come on, don't be a coward.*

"Easy for you to say," I grumbled, climbing off the couch. In the ten-foot walk from the couch to the front door, I tried to smooth my wild hair.

Opening the door, I found him standing there, a large paper cup in each hand. "Hey."

I blinked at him a few times, taking in his hat pulled sloppily over his hair, to the day-old stubble, to his rumpled clothes, to his... *Was that a black eye?*

"What happened to you?"

A paper cup in hand, he touched the corner of his eye with his pinky. "Oh, this. It's no big deal. You should see the other guy."

"I don't think I want to."

He smirked at my comment. Even with his black eyes and what appeared to be a scrape on his neck, he was still unworldly handsome, still devastating me with his gaze. "I was hoping we could talk?"

"Talk," I repeated back stupidly.

"Yeah, I brought you a drink. Lavender London Fog, right?" He handed the drink over to me, the insignia of the local coffee shop on the side. I tried not to let the pang of tenderness go deeper. Not that wild that he remembered my drink order. No big deal.

My hand wrapped around the warm cup, and I nodded at him. "Right."

He stuck his free hand in his pocket and glanced down sheepishly. "Yesterday, before I said all those messed up things, you wanted to talk, and I didn't let you. Can I come in?"

I opened the door fully for him. He walked in, so close I could smell the warm woodsy scent of him and feel his heat. He turned to face me, dark circles under his eyes. Maybe he slept as poorly as I did. Though there was no way he drank as much as I did.

"You leave today?" he asked.

I took a curing sip of my drink. He even remembered I liked a sprinkle of cinnamon on top. "I have to be out by eleven. Though I don't know how I'll drive with all the snow."

"It's pretty bad. I had to go in four-low in a few spots to get up here in time."

"In time?" I asked, wishing I could keep the hope out of my voice. *Did this mean...no. It might not mean a thing.*

"I couldn't have you leave without telling you..." His words broke off, and his brow furrowed as he glanced over my shoulder into the living room. "Is that my dog?"

I grimaced. How had I forgotten about my dognapping? I was planning on smuggling her back in before Adrian got back and then sneaking away. That was before I was useless with a hangover.

"Um. What?" Straining to keep a casual expression on my face, I furrowed my brow and glanced up at the ceiling in innocence.

He cocked his head to the side, walking past me and picking up his dog. She stared up at him, licking his face in greeting. "Did you steal my dog last night?" His tone was confused but not harsh.

I released out a huff of air as if his question was an irritant. "You left her all alone in that big house..."

"It's barely over a thousand square feet."

"And the snow was coming down so heavily and she was hungry and you left her with no way to go potty and..."

"She has a dog door, you know. If she needs to do her business, she knows how to get in and out of the house, and she had plenty of food."

"She was cold," I argued.

A small smile quirked up the corner of his mouth. "She was? In her thick fur? On her mountains of blanket and pillows inside my well-insulated house?"

Hugging myself together, I stared him down. "Yes."

His lips pursed as if he was trying to hold back a laugh, and he nodded at me. "Glad to know she was in good hands."

"I was going to give her back. It's not like I would keep her forever. It was one night, and you didn't come back."

His expression turned solemn, and he let out a loud sigh. "No, I didn't. I ended up having a few too many at the bar last night and crashed on Tam and Penny's couch."

"Oh." I felt silly all of a sudden. We stood in quiet for what felt like five minutes but was probably only fifteen seconds. I tried to imagine what it was he would want to say to me. There was no getting around the fact that I was leaving in a few hours. Nothing was tying me to the town, no matter how much I wanted to stay.

Adrian crouched down, setting Maizie on the floor where she pranced off toward the couch, settling herself into a ball and going to sleep in minutes. With no dog between us, the air felt more charged.

Adrian shoved his hands in his pockets, taking a deep breath as if to summon the courage to say his words. I fought against the rising hope in my chest that they would be what I needed to hear.

"Yesterday, those terrible words I said to you. I didn't mean any of them. I screwed up."

"I was really hurt, and you didn't even hear me out." Until I said the words, I hadn't realized how much I needed to say them. To tell him my truth. This was what I never did with Buck. I couldn't trust him to listen, to learn. But with Adrian, it was crucial he understood I was hurt, that the idea of losing him broke a piece of me I didn't know already belonged to him. "I don't care that it's only been a few days. That there are so many things we don't know about each other because I trusted you with a part of me. And to have that turned around back on me, to be left in the cold by you without a conversation..."

"I know. Maybe I was scared of how I'm feeling, maybe it was all too much too soon. Seeing your rich ex-boyfriend set me off, and I started doubting myself. But none of it was because of you. You didn't deserve my words." He pulled his hat off, bunching it in his fist.

"Thank you for saying that." I wasn't sure I could trust him enough for forgiveness yet.

He ran a hand over his messy hair, matted on one side and sticking up on the other. "Last night, I was a mess. The moment I left you, I knew I was making a mistake, but I didn't know how to fix it. Was too scared to come up here. I kept telling myself that maybe how I was feeling wasn't this powerful. That it couldn't be. A single long weekend wasn't enough to feel this strongly. That eventually I would get over you. But once again, I was wrong. Because I know now. There is no getting over you."

The sound I made was somewhere between a gasp and a shuddering breath. I waited for him to say the words I needed.

"I know that you and Buck have all this history, that he knows you well. That we just met a few days ago, but I can't help but ask you not to go back with him. Give us a chance."

"A chance for what?" I stepped closer. If I leaned forward, I could place a hand on his chest. But I needed him to close the gap, my feet frozen.

A softness grew behind his ocean eyes. "The entire way back up here, I was rehearsing what I would say. How I want to tell you that, from the moment I found you standing on my porch, something changed in me. I don't want the same things anymore. I want more."

"I want it, too," I whispered, and his eyes flashed to mine in surprise and joy. He stepped closer, laying a hand on my cheek and pulling my face up to his. Breaths away, he ran a thumb over my jaw.

"I'm not sure how to be the man you deserve, but I will spend every day giving it all I have to come close. Don't leave. Stay here with me."

"This is crazy. We barely know each other." My eyes were welling with happy tears as I tried one last time to put a semblance of reason into what we had.

A slight smile ticked up on the edge of his mouth. "I know I'm falling in love with you. Am already in love with you. It's sudden, but that doesn't make it wrong. There are a million reasons this is a bad idea, but I don't care. For the first time, I can see exactly what I need in life. I love the way you laugh with a little snort. And the way you rub behind your left ear when you're nervous. I love the way your hair looks like a mushroom when you take off your bonnet in the morning and that spark in your eyes when you meet someone new. Starting now, I want to be everything you need. I don't need to think over every angle, I know. There will never be another woman who affects me the way you do. I'm sure of you."

"I'm sure of you. I think..." I hesitated, knowing the words were right, even when the idea of them was too soon. "I think I'm in love with you, too."

The words were barely out before his lips crashed against mine.

His tongue warred against mine, the kiss punishing as he wrapped his arms around my waist and pulled me close. Even through all the layers of clothes, I could feel the strong length of him. Walking backward, we made it halfway to the stairs before he changed direction, and instead, we ended up in the living room. He hesitated. "I don't have any more condoms...We used them all up already."

Cupping the back of my neck, I steadied him. "I trust you. I have the implant, and I got tested a month ago."

"I've never gone without protection with a woman before."

"I'm your first?" I asked, a smile stretching my lips.

"And the last." His words were strong, his ocean eyes darkening to a storm.

"And the last," I echoed.

He lowered me onto the floor, stripping the layers of winter clothes away. Each article removed accompanied by a kiss of the exposed skin. My wrist, the crook of my elbow, the back of my knee. The brush of his mouth at the center of me and then he was there over me. The lean of his body flush with mine as he kissed me where I needed him the most. My hand in his hair, he worked over me until I was crying out his name.

There was no more to be said, no space between us that hadn't been filled by his apology and my forgiveness.

Wren

R OUND TWO WAS IN the small shower—our elbows and knees knocking against the yellowing tile wall as he held one leg up to thrust deep inside me. Round three was in the bed that hadn't seen even a hair of mine for days. It was hours later, when the sunlight was in the right pot for the upstairs loft, that we heard a truck coming up the drive. Naked, Adrian walked to the small window to peek down below.

"Crap. It's Trudy, the cleaner," he remarked, snagging a pillow off the floor and holding it against his pelvis.

Sitting upright in bed, I glowered at the window. "The cleaner? How the hell did she make it up that hill? It's a blizzard out there."

Another pillow on his butt. He walked sideways to the top of the stairs. "She's very industrious. That's why Agatha hired her. I have to get downstairs and find my clothes before she catches me..."

"Hello!" a craggy voice called as the door swung open with an audible crash. "It's Trudy! Anyone here!"

Adrian's eyes grew wide, and I had to bite back the laugh that was threatening to burst from me. The struggle was so hard, my jaw hurt from the tension before I let out a loud gasp and said, "Yeah, just a minute."

Still holding the pillows against his nether bits, Adrian seethed at me, his words hissing through his teeth in a whisper. "What are you doing? I'm naked over here."

"You have your pillows. Give me a minute, and I'll bring you your clothes." Pulling on the first set of leggings and sweatshirt I could find, I walked barefoot down the stairs to find an older woman with gray hair braided into a coronet.

The woman looked me up and down, frowning. "You're 'posed to be outta here by eleven."

My finger rubbed behind my left ear. "Right, sorry. The storm threw me for a loop."

The woman took her time, glaring from my red-painted toenails to my still-damp hair. She let out an indecipherable noise somewhere between a hum and a snort. "You must be the ex. That boyfriend of yours is a pain in the ass."

"Who?" I asked.

"Burt, Drake, something like that."

"Buck," I corrected, walking to the living room window to see that the spot that previously held his expensive SUV was now empty. At the end of the road, I glimpsed the red brake lights as he turned onto the main mountain road. "How did..."

"Someone at the hotel said he needed a cab up here. I charged him fifty for the ride." She leaned against the counter. "If I knew he was going to be such a whiner, I would have charged his twenty more. I'm no therapist, you know."

"Right." I nodded.

"Look, I don't give a rat's ass about Bart. But I need you out of here so I can get it clean for the next guests."

"Of course. Give me a few, and I'll..."

"Not to interrupt this, but can I get my pants?" Adrian called down.

I forgot he didn't have clothes up there, so shocked by the cleaning lady moonlighting as an emergency taxi service for my ex. Snagging the clothes off the floor, I moved to go up the stairs, but Trudy blocked it.

"That better not be who I think it is. Adrian Winter, what the devil are you doing up there?" She put her hands on her hips and stood at the foot of the stairs, staring up at him. "And can you explain why you're up there but your drawers are down here?" She pronounced drawers like draws.

"Do you really need to ask that, Trudy?" He held the pillow tighter on his front and grimaced. "Can someone throw me my clothes? Birdie, please."

Trying in vain to hide the smirk on my face, I sidestepped Trudy on the stairs to hand a hassled Adrian his belongings. He stepped to the side, dropping the pillow and hastily pulling on his pants. Once the shirt was over his head, he frowned at me. "It's not funny."

Covering my laugh with a cough, I put on a serious expression. "Of course not. Not at all."

"That woman is friends with my family."

"Who isn't in this town?"

On the ground floor, Trudy had her arms crossed against her ample chest. "So, the rumors were true." She narrowed her eyes at his face. "Nice shiner."

Rumors? What was he up to that there would be rumors?

Adrian colored slightly at the comment, giving me a sideways glance. "Uh, yeah. Nothing I couldn't handle."

"That's not what I heard. And I heard all about it, from Jordan, from Marta. And then the guy spent the whole drive up here complaining about you two."

The guy? Wait...

"Buck was the one you fought with last night?"

"We got into a minor disagreement."

"About what?"

"A multitude of things."

"Adrian!"

"What, Birdie? I couldn't have the guy saying shit about my girlfriend."

"Girlfriend?" I startled at the word. Is that what I was? The word felt wrong, but at that moment, it was the least of my concerns. "Whatever, you can't fight with Buck. I already told him I don't want to see him again." I motioned to Trudy. "Thus the reason he was left behind and had to pay fifty dollars to get back here."

Adrian glanced at Trudy, a smirk on his face. "Fifty? I would have charged him a hundred."

"Wish I woulda," Trudy said with a grimace, shaking her head. "Now, I don't care what hanky-panky you two are getting into, but you gotta do it somewhere else. I'll give you ten minutes to gather up your things, and you're outta here."

Adrian nodded at her. "Of course." He turned to me. "Birdie, go pack your stuff up there. I'll grab everything down here, and we'll move it over."

My arms crossed against my chest, I studied him. "To your place? I mean, I guess that will work until I can get my car out of the snow…"

"I don't give a damn about the snow. You'll stay with me and Maizie. Until you want to leave."

"You're asking me to stay?" The words came out breathy, the last string that was holding me back snapping away.

"I am, as long as you'll have me."

Threw my arms around his neck, pulling him close, my lips finding his in a passionate kiss. His hands found my hips, gripping tight as we found each other.

"For the love of Pete! Will you two get your shit together and get out of here so I can clean?" Trudy's voice broke us apart.

Our cheeks reddened, but our smiles didn't waver as we pulled away from each other to gather my things.

Adrian carried all the bags, while I had Maizie tucked into my coat the way I did the night before. Walking into the cabin, it felt like coming to a home I never knew I wanted.

He set my stuff down on the floor beside the door and turned to me. "Do you want something to eat? I could make something if you're hungry."

I shook my head, stepping close to him and wrapping my arms around his waist. His shirt smelled of cedar and soap. Of him. Closing my eyes, I savored the moment, the fabric soft against my cheek and the strength of his forearms holding me tight. "You called me your girlfriend," I murmured into his chest.

I felt his lips on my hair, then his cheek. "I did. Is that okay?"

Nodding into him, I breathed him in one last time before pulling back to stare up at him. "The word doesn't feel right, boyfriend, girlfriend, for us. But it will have to do for a while."

A mischievous grin lit up his face. "A short while."

Snap, snap, snap. Inside my chest were the last tenets of hesitation. I laid my hand against his cheek, rubbing a thumb over the edge of his bruise.

"Take me to bed."

Leaning down, his lips stopped a breath away from mine. His words soft. "I will. But first, can you take back the curse you put on me? I'd like to keep my cattle."

It took me a few minutes to understand his question before I recalled my angry outburst the night before. My face breaking into a grin, I nodded. "I'll see what I can do. No guarantee about the lightning strikes, though."

His lips found mine, beseeching as his kiss deepened. My hands in his hair. The hat tossed to the floor. My shirt, his pants, his shirt, my bra. Once we got to the foot of his stairs, we were half naked, our hands raking over each other. One backward step up, and he was grabbing my naked thighs, pulling me up until my legs were wrapped around his waist. The core of me rubbed against his hard length with every step he took to the bedroom. Sizzling with need, by the time we reached the landing, I was ready for him. A pulse beat inside me, echoing louder as he gently laid me on the bed. Reaching down to my ankles, he placed them on the bed, my legs splayed open. Over my body, his hand wavered, as if in a trance.

"Somehow, you're better each time I see you like this. Open for me, wet, mine."

"Yours," I echoed.

Gently, his hand slid under my ass, pulling my thin lacy thong down over my legs until I was bare for him. His mouth found the apex of my thighs, parting me with his tongue. My hips bucked off the bed, meeting him with a clash. The things his tongue was doing to me, I was edging closer with a few well-placed swipes and hums. His fingers held onto my ass, digging into the flesh to bring me closer to his mouth.

"My sweet, good girl. I thought I'd never see you again, to taste you. So sweet on my tongue as you come." Between words, he licked up my seam, circling my clit. "The feel of you under me, so soft, ready. Mine."

With his own possessive words, I buried my hands in my hair, holding him closer. He found the center of my desire, working his tongue around it, circling and dipping. First slow and languid, then faster as I thrashed against his mouth.

"This cunt is mine. This skin is mine. No one else's."

"No one's," I echoed back. "Only you."

With a smile on his face, he sucked my clit into his mouth, sending me crashing over. Swirls and stars and the fog of explosions behind my eyes. I held him tight to me as I rode the climax down.

"I need you now." Reaching up, I wound my arms around his neck, pulling him down for a kiss. "I need you bare inside me. I need you to be mine."

Cupping my face in his palm, his gaze grew tender. "It's always been you. Even before I met you, some part of me knew. From the moment I saw you standing on the wrong porch, I can't fight it, I can't stop it. I've always been yours."

"Make love to me."

This kiss was tender—silk and sugar. As our bodies came together, it was absolution from all that was before each other. There was only him and I. Only this kiss, the expanse of his back under my hand, and the slide of his skin as he covered my body with his.

His hands gripped mine, pulling them above my head to grip his headboard. "Keep your hands up," he ordered, his tone soft but firm. "No moving them until I tell you to."

His first thrust into me had me gasping, pleasure rocketing through my body. His hands on my hips, his teeth on my collarbone, the rough scrape of his beard on my breast.

"Look at you taking me. You're such a good girl, aren't you? Taking my cock." He stared down between us, at where we were joined. "Taking me so well. You were made for me."

His dirty words were heaven to my ears, spurring me on to move with each thrust. My fingers dug into the wrought iron above me, my muscles tight. "I need to hold you. Let me touch you," I begged.

"Yes, touch me. Love me."

Letting go of the headboard, my hand skated down his back, holding him closer. My legs wrapped around his waist, and I brought my mouth to his. A beautiful agony of wanting more and more to find it all in his touch.

We came together, our eyes open. Each thrust was a possession, mine, mine, mine. I met him each time, our eyes locked. Ours, ours, ours.

This climax was different, softer, somehow. A low ache that built into an expanding chasm inside my chest that only his touch could fill. The blinding light of it arcing through me. It was warmth, safety, and trust. It was love.

Epilogue

Wren

I studied the group text that Summer sent to all of us, inspecting the picture of some generic woman holding up her left hand beside the man we all thought was Summer's boyfriend. The texts start piling in.

I sent a quick one of my own.

Since I never met the man, this was conjecture, but still. We sent a few more vague threats before Summer announced she was about to land at SeaTac. Knowing her, she paid extra to compulsively scroll through Cory's Instagram. While the rest of us weren't capable of more than half-hearted threats, Summer was a force. I briefly pondered if I should tell her dad to keep an eye on her before she committed a felony. The woman made our middle school math teacher cry in the middle of class once. Who knew what she would do if in this situation.

I typed out a quick message and started to scroll through my contacts to find Mr. Townsend, when Adrian called out from the bedroom.

"Birdie, come up here."

I set my phone down and sidestepped Maizie, who was always under my feet, to walk up the stairs to our bedroom.

While we were crazy for one another, I wasn't crazy enough to move in with him after a single weekend. Once we untangled from each other to find food, we talked out the logistics. The move back to my parents' house was hard. Adrian came and visited me every weekend for a month before I decided it was too much for both of us. I didn't want Ridgewood, with its steeple church overlooking the bay and the beautifully painted storefronts. I wanted Icicle Creek, with its chipped door bar and doily-covered diner. I wanted Adrian.

Marta, at the diner, offered to let me rent out the small apartment in her basement for six months. While I could have kept working for Andra Data, I quit a few months in to start my own business coaching job. I worked with several local businesses, including Tam and Penny's store, the diner, and The Horse and Trails. The majority of my work was still completed remotely or I had to travel, but I didn't mind that anymore. Working for myself, seeing my recommendations put into effect, was a far more rewarding experience. I wasn't making half as much, but it didn't matter with Adrian by my side. I wasn't afraid of the adventure of other places when I knew I had a home waiting for me.

Adrian asked me to move in a month after I agreed to stay, but I told him we should wait. Then, another month later, he asked again. I relented after three months together. Marta was kind enough to let me break our handshake lease.

The snow melted from the yard, and the river raged on loudly from the new water. Small purple crocus pushed up through the brown dirt to welcome the sun. I took up gardening, something I had never known could be so exciting. On rainy days, I could be found curled on the couch, researching the right locations for sun exposure and the timing of planting and harvesting. I made spreadsheets, drew diagrams, and settled into life at the cabin.

On the second floor, I joined Adrian, who was standing in front of our dresser in only his boxers, a pair of shorts in his hand. He had his back to the window and his eyes covered. "Is that what I think it is?" He motioned across the street to Agatha's cabin.

"Are people having sex in the hot tub again?" I asked.

In the months since I found that the upstairs window of the cabin had a direct sight line to the hot tub, at least once a week, we would glance out the window and find a couple getting it on in the hot water. The first few times, it was funny. Now it was more like an odd backdrop to our lives.

"Not exactly..."

I joined him at the window and then took a quick step back. "Is that..."

"I think so."

Across the street, naked as the day, sat Marta, Trudy, and Agatha in the hot tub, oversized glasses of wine in their hands and cackling like banshees.

Adrian stepped back. "I'm blinded. Those women were like grandmothers to me. I can't believe I just saw their boobs."

"Well, maybe not their boobs. The water is high, and the boobs are saggy."

Adrian sank into the bed. "I'm traumatized. Utterly wrecked."

I glanced one more time at the window. All three ladies looked up at me, waving as if they didn't have a care in the world. I waved back. "I think they know you can see them."

"That's worse."

"Worse than being a peeper?"

"I didn't mean to look over there. I was getting dressed and glanced out and…" He shook his head. "Didn't I tell Agatha to build a privacy screen? I even offered to split the cost."

I laughed at him. "They don't seem too bothered by it."

"Well, I am! I have no interest in watching naked people in the hot tub."

"We both know that isn't quite true. You sure watched me for a while when I was over there."

"That was different. It was you and…"

"And?" Throwing a leg on each side of his legs, I straddled his lap, rubbing myself against him. My sundress rose on my thighs.

His hands ventured under my dress, cupping my bare ass. "Are you not wearing underwear?"

"I forgot." I ground myself against the front of him.

Stealing a kiss, he laced his hands in my curls, holding me tight. I reached between us, pulling his boxers down to free his hard cock. Stroking down the length of him once, we were both ready. Bare to him, I placed my hands on his shoulders, lifting myself until he could sink inside me. Together, we moved, our faces inches from each other. Each stoke reminded me how much he loved me. Bringing his face to mine, I kissed him without abandon. He tugged the front of my dress down, freeing my breast. Bringing one nipple into his mouth, his tongue circled the tip, his teeth scraping against the tender flesh there as I held tight to his hair, urging for more, harder, faster. This was quick. We found our release in minutes, with me coming first and him following right behind me. His hands gripped my hips as we cried out together. Falling back, I rolled to the side of him, a laugh escaping both of us as we stared at one another.

"I love you, Birdie."

I couldn't imagine a world where those words would give me a thrill to hear, each time just as powerful as the first.

"I love you more."

"I'm never going to tire of being inside you. Having you is all I could ever want."

I turned my head to look at him, a smile playing on my lips. "That may be true, but I think I need a little break. I don't know if I have any more orgasms in me."

A wicked grin lit up his face. "Wanna bet?" he asked before capturing my mouth with his.

Acknowledgements

Thank you to

My family for not always reading my books but always encouraging me to write them. My boys who can never read these books.

Cassidy for being my first reader.

My husband for everything under the sun, but specifically for explaining without sounding condescending; the mechanics of how to tow a car, and how four-low works in the snow.

Thank you to my RAWR girls; Laura, Kate, Shannon, Greta Rose, MJ, and Dillon, for always having a funny picture, words or encouragement, or the advice that yes, naked is the right word to use—Aperol Spritzes and Bub the Bear hugs all around.

And as always to my wonderful readers for loving my stories as much as I do.

About the Author

Linnea March is a contemporary romance author who writes steamy stories about self-confident women and the rugged men who love them. She lives somewhere in the wilds of the Pacific Northwest with her husband, their two boys, and a plump dog. After fifteen years of teaching early childhood education, she put down the googly eyes and picked up a pen. When not writing, she can be found reading her way through an ever-growing pile of books while drinking copious amounts of coffee. She proudly refuses to use umbrellas.